JOURNEY

Liz Garnett

Dedicated to my sons

This book would not have been possible without the support of my friends and family. I have also been lucky enough to meet some fascinating people on my personal journey.

Journey by Liz Garnett

First published in February 2020 by Beechthorpe Press

www.lizgarnett.com

Artwork credits: Liz Garnett

ISBN: 978-0-9935603-4-7

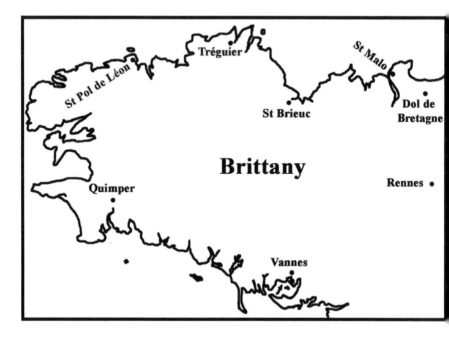

Aggie and Miles follow the route of the Tro Breiz pilgrimage around Brittany. This route visits the sites of the seven founding saints of Brittany:

Vannes – Saint Pattern
Quimper – Saint Corentin
Saint Pol de Léon – Saint Pol Aurélien
Tréguier – Saint Tugdual
Saint Brieuc – Saint Brieuc
Saint Malo – Saint Malo
Dol de Bretagne – Saint Samson

Further details about this route can be found at: www.trobreiz.com

Week 1 – Day 1 - Kent

What had induced Aggie to book the 6.20 am ferry from Dover escaped her as she sped down the M20 motorway towards the ferry port. The car had been hurriedly packed the night before and was still unwashed. Mud was caked on the wheel arches and up the sides of the doors from months of rural driving.

Aggie was anxious about this trip, her first without her eldest son. Richard was safely tucked up in bed planning his end-of-school holiday and, in particular, relishing the opportunity to throw wild parties while his mother and younger brother were away. Miles was also anxious. Being in sole charge of his mother weighed heavily on his mind. It wouldn't be the same without Richard to lead him astray. The M20 became the A20 and as the car headed down the hill towards Dover he thought of the fun he had had with Richard on previous holidays.

Trips to French supermarkets were usually fun. There was less pressure to behave as they wouldn't bump into anyone they knew and embarrass their mother. Aggie was a bit of a hippy in all but dress sense. This changed the minute she left the UK with her conventional smart casual clothing being left behind in favour of a more relaxed look of ancient shorts, frayed jeans and much loved relics from her art college days. She felt a huge amount of pressure to appear to conform. Having been single for twelve years she was acutely aware of the negative stereotyping of single mothers. She had no objection to her sons using cucumbers as lightsabres in the vegetable aisles of the supermarkets in France – as long as they added any damaged ones to the trolley. However, at home it was a different matter after she had overheard a couple of local mothers discussing her relaxed parenting style. Since then, she had found ways of avoiding taking the boys shopping. She was determined

5

not to prove these narrow-minded harridans right in their belief that her sons would end up with low grades at school and on drugs to boot. This didn't mean that she was following in their example of being a pushy mother. It was that her style was to guide her children and lead by example when it came to studying. She believed in management rather than control.

Miles' mind was savouring in the delights of past holiday fun with Richard. He thought back to the time when Richard had shown him condoms in the small Carrefour Market at Saint Valery sur Somme. It had been such a giggle to pile up the shopping basket with them and run up to his mother saying in a loud voice "Maman, I didn't know how many you wanted, so I got the lot." Both boys had been bent double with the giggles. Luckily, Aggie had laughed. Immediately giving the boys the opportunity to say: "you laughed! We're off the hook." As always, this prompted Aggie to rue the day she had allowed the boys to watch The Simpsons as this was one of Homer's favourite sayings. Aggie had been grateful for her sunglasses which had masked her embarrassment. She had been pleased to see her boys discovering their 'free child' and finding entertaining ways to be creative.

Miles was brought back into the moment as the car came to the first roundabout on the outskirts of Dover. Smoke had started to issue from the bonnet of the car. He hoped it wasn't serious.

"Shit," said Aggie. "That's all I need."

Pulling into the next petrol station she lifted the bonnet to see what was going on. It appeared that the oil that hadn't made it into the oil tank, when she was filling it up the night before, was smoking nicely on the hot engine. It didn't look too dangerous so she closed the bonnet and headed onto the port.

Journey by Liz Garnett

Aggie hated the Port of Dover with a deep and sincere loathing. It wasn't obvious which lane she should drive in and she really didn't want to end up driving around and through the security check-in by mistake. The horror of having someone go through her badly packed car, disrupting what little organisation there was in it was almost too much to bear. In addition to this she was acutely aware that she was already running late for the ferry.

After passing through the border checks and going past the security checkpoint, the single lane for car traffic opened up into a multitude of lanes joined by the freight traffic. The overhead gantries indicating the different ferry companies was not the easiest to follow. This was where, every year, the arguments started. Miles knew best and Aggie was being a moron if she couldn't see where they were supposed to be. It was obvious wasn't it? He moaned at her about her ineptitude. How, she wondered, was an elderly woman meant to find her way to France? She could see herself in 30 years' time causing complete havoc trying to find the right lane. She would be lucky if she even got on the right ferry.

Spying another car, Aggie pulled in behind it at the ferry company booth and within minutes she was giving her name and then being told which lane to join. With the lane number hanger dangling from her rear view mirror she pulled away from the booth. The stress of finding her way around the port had her immediately forgetting what lane number she was meant to find.

"What lane are we in again?" she asked as she followed the arrows directing traffic to the ferries.

"149."

"Oh God! Where is that?"

"Over there!"

"Where?"

"Are you blind or something? There! There!" shouted an exasperated Miles pointing to the number 149 painted at the end of one queue. What planet was his mother on?

"Oh right, thank you. It is not easy to see where you need to go when you have got lorries coming up behind you at speed."

"Yes it is! Are you blind?"

"You try driving!"

"I will be better than you! The lane is over there!"

"This one?"

"No! Not that one! Are you really that dense? The number is painted at the end of the queue."

"Oh, I didn't see that as I was looking up at the overhead numbers and if you carry on like this we will go straight home!"

Aggie much preferred the road system at the Eurotunnel terminal as there was no chance for mistakes. Concrete lane dividers and 'lifty barrier things' saw to that. She wondered whether the designer of the Eurotunnel road system had had elderly parents or had grown up on a farm where he had had to herd sheep.

They had half an hour to wait before boarding so Aggie took the time to look around at the other travellers. There were a lot of clean and shiny cars. None of them were smoking either. Part of her hoped that some helpful man would come and check under the bonnet of her car and assure her that nothing was wrong with it. Sadly no help was forthcoming so she took the lid off her thermos of coffee and started her daily fix of super strength coffee while Miles stared grumpily out of the window while plugged into the music on his smartphone. Aggie was thankful, for once, that Richard wasn't there for Miles to pick a fight, engage in an argument or worse. There had been numerous arguments in the ferry queue over the years. Travelling was stressful for them all but France, when they got there, was an escape and this year she had intended it to be a pilgrimage of sorts.

Having supported her eldest son to the point of university and put work on hold she now felt lost. Inspiration wasn't forthcoming and she just couldn't come up with any new ideas for paintings. She desperately needed a new style. Her current working practice had become stale. No matter what she tried: oils, pastels, printmaking, watercolours. Nothing gave her the buzz she needed to proceed. Subject matter was also a problem. She had made a name for herself with detailed oil paintings of fruit and flowers. Now still life didn't excite her as it once had. Portraits were tempting but she didn't fancy the idea of taking commissions as the whole process made her physically sick. The worry of whether a client would like the end result was a fundamental hurdle preventing her from undertaking commissions. If they didn't like the picture that would have an effect on potential future commissions.

With Miles listening to music, Aggie used the current moment of calm to open the car door and take in the smell of the air: a mixture of sea salt and diesel fumes. Seagulls floated on the air and called out to their friends. One landed on the bonnet of the car and Aggie watched it watching her. She was reminded of her chickens. Until, that is, Miles tapped the window and it flew off. Looking out of the window she then looked at the queues of traffic and holidaymakers. It appeared that she was the only one who hadn't cleaned her car before embarking on this cross channel journey. Why, she pondered, did people clean their cars in advance of a holiday? Most of her fellow holidaymakers would be travelling a fair distance and in her experience it wouldn't be long before the car would be filthy. She reflected on her first holidays as a single mother and the amount of raisins and breadsticks that managed to find their way underneath the boys car seats. It had been quite revolting. Mucking out the car was a six monthly activity and there was no way Aggie was going to embark on it immediately before it was guaranteed to get gungy within days. It wasn't that she was lazy – she was time poor and had more sense. She had no intention of spending the holiday getting stressed because she had just cleaned the car.

Eventually, the queue started to move and they were on the ferry. There were a lot of cars already on the car deck before Aggie was directed to park up. This didn't bode well. Opening her car door she could smell damp oil and the stench of stale urine. Bracing herself for the packed ferry, she took a deep breath, which she immediately regretted, and got out of the car.

Once upstairs they battled through the crowds to find a quiet spot to sit and eat their breakfast. This was definitely not cruising across the channel as had once been promised in the old ferry company adverts. Miles was in a world of his own looking out of the window and Aggie reflected on past holidays. She remembered the times they had been through the Channel Tunnel and the boys had run around the car deck. Those were the times when she felt it necessary to wear a headscarf and dark glasses just in case someone recognised her. This was one of the drawbacks to living so close to a channel port. Locals would regularly cross to Europe on either the Folkestone/Calais or the Dover/Calais route. The boys had had fun running up to the security camera making rude faces and doing rude signs. Back then she had hoped that whoever was watching the security feed was enjoying their entertaining behaviour as much as she was. She had given up pretending she wasn't amused. They always made her laugh. Another of their entertaining activities had been to push their faces up against the passenger window. Miles felt it necessary to get as much of his face, including his tongue squished up against the window. And the results were hysterical. Richard would wind the window up and down and once nearly caught Miles' tongue in the process. Over the years Aggie had learnt to ignore the horrified looks of strangers and it was a relief that no one locally had seen the antics of her sons – she hoped. It was hard work living in a village and trying to give the impression that she was bringing up her sons according to societal norms.

When the boys had been younger, criticism had been directed at her by one of the village busy bodies. Because she was an artist, the married mother had felt the need to suggest that her sons had seen a large number of naked bodies because as an artist "that was what she painted." Aggie had been so taken aback by the comment that it had rendered her speechless. The woman in question had clearly never seen her work as Aggie never painted nudes. As a single mother, she found that it was immediately assumed that she had no control over her children and they lived off burgers and chips. Even the broadsheet newspapers were reporting on the high consumption of chips and junk food by the children of single mothers. This enraged Aggie as she only fed her boys home cooked food. It had seemed, at the time, that it was 'open season' for having a go at single mothers.

Aggie had read a lot of books on psychology and child rearing. Some advice she ignored, some she adapted and some she embraced wholeheartedly. She encouraged her sons to embrace their inner child and this had resulted in lots of fun at home. From time to time they would jump out on each other and shout "boo". This resulted in lots of screaming – Aggie being one of the loudest. In-house water fights occurred from time to time and she didn't dare have a lie in for fear of a cold wet flannel being rubbed in her face while in slumber.

Suddenly, her mobile rang disturbing her meandering thoughts. It was her boyfriend, Doug. She immediately felt deflated. This was becoming a more and more common feeling when he rang. Since meeting him a year earlier he had increasingly monopolised her free weekends. She wasn't sure how this had come about. She felt partly to blame as, early on, she had got caught up in the buzz of a new relationship. Looking back on it she was beginning to realise that she had been in love with the idea of being loved. Doug was increasingly giving her the impression of not being in love with her. In fact she was becoming increasingly convinced that he was still in love with his ex-wife. Of course, he denied this when questioned.

Doug was phoning to extol the virtues of his villa in the south of France: sea views, spacious rooms, a pool and a short drive from the centre of Saint Tropez. Oh, how she would have loved the villa, he kept reminding her. She should have gone with him, he said. Not on your nelly, she thought. She was not going to subject Miles to the horrors of his two children. She also hadn't wanted to be the subject of his eldest daughters' bitchy twitter feed for two weeks. Both girls were on a mission to get their parents reunited and Doug wasn't helping matters by asking "how high" when his ex-wife said "jump".

Journey by Liz Garnett

Aggie looked around her at the heaving mass of sweaty travellers pushing and shoving their way around the crowded ferry. Silently she groaned and looked out of the window at the approaching coastline of France. Almost there, she thought. She muttered to Doug that she had to go and hung up.

Eventually, the tannoy announced the arrival of the ferry in Calais and requested that all car and lorry drivers make their way down to their vehicles. Waiting until the majority of the passengers had made their way down to the car deck, Aggie and Miles collected their bags and headed down to their car. Aggie's mind was focussed on remembering to drive on the French side of the road at the same time as wondering why no crew member had shown the slightest concern in a car that had a smoking bonnet.

Escaping the Port of Calais was remarkably easy and the port exit flowed seamlessly onto the A16 autoroute and south towards Boulogne. Aggie braved the viaduct at Boulogne with her heart in her mouth. She hated big bridges and this one had her griping the steering wheel and staying resolutely in the fast lane so that she could see as little as possible of the bridge as it curved around. She most certainly did not want to see the valley below. Once over this her hands and shoulders relaxed and she started to enjoy the changing scenery.

Aggie's anxiety levels started to rise again as she drove down the A28 autoroute as she wanted to make sure she got off at the junction for the A29 autoroute and Le Harvre. She wasn't going to think about the very big bridge, although it was there at the forefront of her mind.

Once on the A29 her attention was focussed on getting off this motorway and onto the road for Lillebonne. Time seemed to stand still as she sped down the autoroute. Adrenaline was pumping through her veins as she worried about missing the Lillebonne junction as the Pont de Normandie, further down the autoroute, was the one bridge she never wanted to make the mistake of ending up on – as a driver or a passenger. She had been on it once before as a passenger and even now she could feel the sensation of the car on the bridge going up and up, seemingly forever, before going over the mid-point and then downwards.

Once she was off the autoroute it was a simple case of following her nose downhill past Lillebonne and into the Seine valley. She drove past the oil refinery on her left and straight to the little ferry crossing. This was what she liked. A break in the journey. A chance to take a deep breath and relax. In the past this crossing had been one of the highlights for her sons. It added to the adventure.

The ferry arrived and, once unloaded, started loading cars and vans heading to Quillebeuf sur Seine. Once on the ferry, Miles and Aggie got out of the car and took photos of each other. Aggie pointed to the sign on a big metal box on the side of the ferry. It read 'Brassieres de Sauvetage'. They giggled at the private family joke and separately visualised enormous life-saving bras. Aggie's eccentric elderly aunt, Betty, had always referred to bra's as 'brassieres' and even to this day this caused childish amusement in Aggie.

Once off the ferry it was relatively easy for Aggie to be guided by the sat nav all the way to Vannes.

She did wonder what planet she was on thinking that she would have the energy to drive all the way to southern Brittany in one day. She had done a similar length journey eight years earlier, but she was younger then. Hitting the 50 milestone in age had made her sit up and start to evaluate her life. Well, at least the long journey would give her that opportunity. Although Miles and Aggie talked from time to time while she was driving, there was still ample time for reflection.

Aggie was spending the last of her savings to fund the trip. It was supposed to give her perspective on the future. Thanks to a good friend, Sally who lived in France, she had been sent a book on the Tro Breiz pilgrimage route for her birthday. Inside the second hand book Sally had written 'here's something to inspire you!' It had been just what she needed. Here was a clearly defined pilgrimage route around Brittany. It was perfect. The route had been created in the middle ages for Breton pilgrims to visit the seven sacred sites of the seven founding saints of Brittany.

The book had arrived a month before the school holidays. Neither Miles nor Aggie had had the chance to get fit, so Aggie had decided that this particular pilgrimage would be completed by car and by travelling along the slower roads once they had reached Vannes.

Her mission, she had decided, was to come back with new ideas for her art or certainly a new career direction as well as some radical answers as to how she wanted to live her life. In essence she wanted to come back a new woman – how hard could that be?

Driving along the A84 past the Aire de la Baie, she hoped she could keep her legs crossed until she reached the Carrefour supermarket just beyond Avranches. Heading down the hill she caught glimpses of Le Mont Saint Michel in the far distance. Her hands were starting to ache. Taking her left hand off the steering wheel she shook it and then repeated the action with her right hand. She took a deep breath and rotated her shoulders. Not much further and she would come off at the Carrefour junction, fill up with petrol and have a pee. She reminded herself that she needed to check the oil as her car had so many things wrong with it that an oil leak wasn't out of the question.

The dashboard was registering an outside air temperature of 30°C. The lack of air conditioning was not a problem while the car was moving. She hoped it wouldn't overheat or break down. The car had been bought brand new with a view to it lasting at least 10 years. At 8 years old, Aggie was aware that there was little or no chance of it passing its MOT in three months' time. 'Constance', as the car had been named, was proving to be a constant pain. She really should have given it a better name but had originally thought that Constance might prove to be constantly reliable rather than a mechanical nightmare.

The outside air temperature continued to rise as they headed down the autoroute towards the Rennes Rocade. By the time they hit the Rocade it had reached 34°C. Luckily for Aggie and Miles the traffic was moving freely. In years gone by, when Aggie had reached the Rocade earlier in the day, the traffic had been stop start stop start all along the ring road. It had been a nightmare with both of the boys bored rigid and fractious and both under 10 years old. She was relieved that she had now hit it at a good time of day. She was already exhausted and desperate for a coffee and something to eat.

Thankfully, they were soon off the Rocade and at the Vannes exit. Within minutes they found a Burger King. As far as Aggie was concerned, this was not a fast food restaurant, but an international chain of public conveniences that also served coffee and chips.

Journey by Liz Garnett

Having consumed two espressos and eaten four large fries between them, they got into the car. Aggie was cursing herself for thinking she could drive all the way to Vannes in one day.

"Ready to rock and roll?" asked Aggie.

"Yup. All strapped in," came the reply.

Looking at the sat nav which indicated the arrival time at the campsite, Aggie turned to Miles.

"We are going to need to floor it in order to get there before reception closes."

"No problem," said Miles, turning to look at his phone. He pressed the YouTube app and searched for some music to aid Aggie's driving.

By the time Aggie had pulled out onto the main road Bonnie Tyler's 'I need a hero' was blasting out of the car speakers.

"Any good?" enquired Miles.

"Yes, but it needs to be a bit faster," came Aggie's reply.

Fiddling with the YouTube settings Miles sped up the music to a faster pace and Aggie could at last feel the adrenalin coursing through her veins.

One hour and ten minutes later, they pulled off the autoroute. Aggie's eyes were wide open and had a manic look resembling a meerkat on steroids. The wind blowing through the open window had blown her hair into a mad mess of tangles.

"Phew," she said at last. "Can we have something a bit more sedate for the local roads?" Having had 'I need a hero' on a loop since Rennes she needed something that would help with a slower and calmer speed required for off motorway driving. She also needed to slow down her heart rate.

By the time they arrived at the campsite it was 8 pm. Aggie was beyond shattered. What on earth was she thinking when she was planning this trip? She pulled up the car in the parking space beside the reception and stiffly got out of the car. She was hot and sweaty from the drive and the outside air still retained the heat of the day. She shook her legs and unstuck the fabric of her shorts that were glued to her legs before heading to the reception.

Luckily there was only a short queue at reception which would give her more time to 'wind down' after the mad drive there and to compose a group text to Magda, Richard and her aunt Betty.

Aggie – Arrived safely in Vannes.

Richard – Ta.

Betty – Well done! I have checked up on Richard and fed him tonight.

Magda – Have a great holiday! Missing you already – especially our 'coffee mornings'!

Aggie smiled at the thought of their 'coffee mornings' and how they would sit in the kitchen enjoying strong black coffee while chatting about the art industry and plotting ways to improve their income. Magda's style of art was very different from Aggie's but from time to time they would come together for joint exhibitions.

They shared business knowledge and shared in the highs and lows of each other's careers.

Within minutes Aggie was signed in and had been given directions to their 'emplacement'. Driving through the campsite down a hill they found the pitch easily with its hedge border. Greeting the English couple in the next door pitch with a "hello" they began unearthing the tent from the car.

The tent was brand new. Aggie didn't believe in doing a trial run of erecting the tent at home before the trip. She wasn't stupid. She knew of the difficulties of trying to squeeze the tent back into it's bag. She also knew that this meant that she had to have extra supplies of guy ropes and pegs just in case. She also didn't believe in reading instructions. So, they set about pulling the tent out of its bag and laying it out on the ground with the opening facing down the hill.

Seeing the difficulty Aggie was having with working out which pole went into which sleeve, the Englishman at the neighbouring pitch offered to help. Seeing as it was getting late, Aggie decided it would be prudent to accept his offer. She was confident that she could erect the tent single-handed but she was tired and Miles was grumpy and in need of food.

With an extra person helping, it made the whole process much easier.

"I am impressed that you are so calm when putting up the tent," said the man.

"Oh, thank you." In Aggie's experience, shouting at her children was fruitless and made the whole camping experience a living hell. So, she did whatever the boys didn't want to do. They would all come home happier and more willing to go on holiday the following year. She also found that the boys pitched in more and were willing to help with the cooking and clearing up.

"I camp a lot and I have heard lots of arguments when people have been putting up their tents," said the Englishman.

Later that night Aggie heard arguments coming from the other tent. Clearly the man's girlfriend hadn't been happy with him helping her put up her tent. What a shame he was attached, thought Aggie. Helpful men like him were hard to find.

At 10.30 pm the campsite entertainment was still in full swing. To Aggie, it sounded as if the band had pumped up the volume and this was all she needed when she was desperate for a good night's sleep. Aggie wasn't keen on campsite entertainment. She had her books and they had playing cards and good communication skills. What more did they need? Oh why hadn't she booked a pitch on a smaller site she thought to herself.

Then, to her horror, as she was trying to mentally block out the band, 'I need a hero' took over at speed whizzing around her head like a rat on amphetamines.

Week 1 – Day 2 - Vannes

Aggie had spent a restless night. It was cold and had rained heavily. The airbed was uncomfortable and she found she had had to keep pumping it up every hour or so during the night. This was a delicate operation because if she pumped the pump hard it made a terrible squeaking sound, so she had had to do the pumping slowly and carefully. The damp also had her going to the toilet four times in the night. The putting on of her skirt over her pyjama bottoms and then her feet into dew soaked flip flops was tiresome and exhausting.

By 7 am the mattress had fully deflated and Aggie had had enough. A long hot shower was just what she needed followed by a hot coffee and some croissants she had brought over from England.

Aggie hated this part of camping. The shower block was cold and the cubicles were small and it was difficult to keep her clean clothes dry. She stood under the blast of hot water and started to wash her hair. The water stopped and she had to push the timer button again to get another blast of hot water. She had to do this repeatedly before she was clean and then she continued pushing the button in order to warm herself up.

Taking a deep breath she grabbed her thin microfibre camping towel and started to dry herself. The towel was almost useless at drying her but was great for packing as it took up so little space so she tried hard to ignore the pitfalls of the fabric. Once dried she wrapped the towel around her lower half and put her arms through the straps on her clean bra, pushed her breasts into the bra cups and then pulled the bra strap around her back. It wouldn't meet in the middle. She took a deep breath in and then exhaled and tried again. No luck. The dampness of her back meant that the fabric of the bra

21

strap wouldn't slide around her back. She tried again but no luck. By this time she was getting more than a little frustrated. She then remembered how she had been taught to put on a bra when she was a teenager. Her arms came out of the arm straps and she pulled the bra around so the fastenings were on her front. She did them up. Perfect. Then she tried to slide the bra around her chest so the fastenings were at the back. No such luck. Her back was still damp. The bra just wouldn't budge. She took the bra off again and pulled the straps to stretch the elastic. She tried again to put the bra on with the fastenings at the back and she finally managed to get the last hooks into the loops. What an ordeal, she thought to herself. She felt exhausted. Mercifully the rest of getting dressed was simpler and ten minutes later she was walking back down the hill to her tent.

Aggie saw that in the time she had been in the shower, the English couple had packed up and left. Oh dear, thought Aggie, the row must have been more serious than it had appeared as the man had talked of spending another couple of days on the campsite.

Miles was still fast asleep having been lucky enough to have the only puncture free airbed.

Aggie started her breakfast routine by getting out the gas stove and placing it on the ground. She placed the saucepan on the stove and added just enough water for her morning coffee. Kneeling in front of the stove she leant forward and tried to ignite the gas. But there was none. This was all she needed.

There was nothing for it but to boot Miles out of bed and head to the Carrefour supermarket that she had seen on the way to the campsite the night before and find a café there for breakfast. Thankfully, Miles had washed the night before. So, it was just a matter of encouraging him to get out of bed, go to the toilet and get dressed before coaxing him into the car.

Aggie retraced their route back to the autoroute junction where she had spotted the Carrefour supermarket. She was relying on her knowledge of French supermarkets and how the larger ones were usually part of a shopping mall complex which included cheap eateries. Their luck was in and they found a place selling croissants and waffles.

"Perfect," she said when she saw the restaurant.

"Can I have a waffle?" asked Miles, hoping that his mother was in a generous mood.

"Yes," came the reply. 'Result,' thought Miles.

Miles found a table while Aggie went up to the counter to order and pay. Miles watched his mother place the order and chat to the woman behind the counter. He could see that she was more relaxed than when they were in Kent. Her freshly washed hair was still damp and this dampness helped to hid the greying of her hair. Looking at her he realised that her hair had become much greyer over the past year. He then turned his attention to her clothing. She was wearing a pair of loose fitting 'hippy' trousers and a tie die t-shirt that she had designed in a fit of rebellion against Doug.

She had bought five white t-shirts from Tesco and gone to work creating interesting tie die patterns after Doug had spent an evening criticising her normal Kent wardrobe of Boden clothes. She hadn't been quite sure what he had expected her to wear. Boden clothes are respectable but perhaps he wanted her to wear more neutral colours. Her Boden clothing was, for the most part, bright and cheerful, reflecting her positive disposition.

Doug had not been impressed when they had next met up again for a pub lunch. Miles smiled as he remembered helping her with the tie-dying. It had been fun encouraging his mother to wind up Doug. Miles didn't like Doug but had been too polite to say anything to Aggie. Doug had barely spoken two sentences to Miles or Richard since he had first met them. Doug had deserved the embarrassment of being seen with Aggie in her tie-dye ensemble.

Watching Aggie from the vantage point of the table, Miles had not been surprised by Doug's shock on seeing Aggie in her new 'outfit'. Aggie looked like an art student who had aged prematurely.

Having tracked down a new mattress, gas canisters and some non-perishable food in Carrefour, Aggie and Miles then headed to the centre of Vannes. Aggie hated driving into new towns but felt more confident with the sat nav guiding her. Miles was far too busy listening to music and staring out of the window to be of assistance. His mind was on food and trying to work out how he could persuade his mother to stop for a coffee and a cake so soon after breakfast.

The roads into the town centre were wide and the traffic was free flowing and before long they found themselves at the marina and the underground parking. Aggie had a dislike of multi-storey and underground parking. She avoided them whenever she could but told herself that it was good to challenge her fears, and as this was a pilgrimage, this was part of the process. Besides, she had found this parking easily and it looked like it was conveniently situated for walking into town.

Coming out of the damp and musty underground parking, they walked into the Place Gambetta and stood looking up at the Porte

Saint Vincent. Behind them, the masts of the sailing boats clinked in the light breeze. The clouds were starting to clear and the damp air felt refreshing. Tourists milled around in front of the entrance to the old town and the restaurants which hugged the town walls. Aggie and Miles walked through Porte Saint Vincent and into Rue Saint Vincent. The architecture looked relatively modern and they continued on up the street and through Place des Lices where the buildings were starting to look more interesting.

Continuing up the hill into Rue de la Monnaie they marvelled at the medieval architecture. Miles extracted his phone from his pocket and started to take pictures. Aggie rummaged in her bag for her small point and shoot camera and did the same. She wished she had a phone that took better pictures but her budget wouldn't stretch that far.

They spent a happy hour wandering around the medieval streets, photographing and enjoying the historic atmosphere. Aggie wondered at the style of buildings and why some of them had overhanging upper floors.

Miles wondered how he could surreptitiously take photos of pretty girls while looking like he was photographing the street or architecture. He wished he was better at drawing people – in particular girls. There might be some merit in this style of art for getting a girlfriend, he thought. Aware of what Miles was doing, Aggie smiled to herself and gently grabbed his arm and directed him back down the hill towards the car.

"I want to nip into the Halle aux Poissons for some prawns for lunch and then get a baguette," said Aggie.

"Oooh," said Miles thinking of food and feeling as though he hadn't eaten in months. "Can we get a cake or something as well?"

"Of course."

Once back at the campsite and having prepared the lunchtime meal Aggie sat down in the low camping chair and took a deep breath. She wanted to savour the meal. Miles switched off his phone and took out his earplugs. He too was looking forward to lunch. Aggie bit into the large prawns which had been dipped in her own mix of mayonnaise, crushed garlic and lemon juice. The flavour pinged around her mouth. This was what she liked. Simple food that was full of flavour. A ripe tomato bought at a market stall had more taste and interest for Aggie than an expensive meal out. It wasn't just the simple ingredients that captivated her. It was also the process of preparing a meal. To her it was almost spiritual, meditative even. The rinsing of the fruit and vegetables mixed with the sound of cutting into a fresh pepper and the smell that then drifted up to her nostrils. These combined with the smell of fresh garlic as she crushed it and the waft of lemon as she cut a fresh, thick skinned lemon in half. It was magical. The freshly baked baguette from the boulangerie would then be torn into pieces and used to mop up the remaining garlic mayonnaise. Aggie was in heaven.

After a peaceful afternoon on the campsite playing cards and sketching, Miles and Aggie nipped into the little mini supermarket in the village. Once back at the campsite, they then settled into their low camping chairs and lit the camp stove. Miles was in charge of supper and tipped six merguez sausages into the frying pan and started to cook them. Aggie broke the fresh baguette into quarters and using her fingers opened up the quarters of baguette down the middle. She took a deep breath and inhaled the spicy smell of the merguez sausages. The smell brought back memories of past holidays when the three of them would take the camp stove to the beach and they would eat sausage baguettes in between making sand castles. Aggie thought back to one of those times when they had been joined by other young children and their fathers in creating an extended fortification in the sand. Aggie had chatted amiably with the fathers until she had become aware of angry looks by the mothers who were sitting sunning themselves.

When the sausages were cooked, Miles put them in the baguette and they sat back and bit into the sausage baguette and savoured the piquancy of the sausage as its juices oozed into the bread. Bliss. Aggie then poured out some of the organic Carrefour cider into their plastic beakers and they then went on to savour the fresh taste of French cider. It wasn't quite as good as local farm cider but it would do.

Before they had a chance to continue with their meal, a group of French teenagers came up to them and asked for some "alcool".

"English," came Aggie's swift reply, knowing that at times like this, there was an advantage of pretending not to speak French.

"Cidre," came the reply, in an attempt not to be deterred.

"No speaky French," tried Aggie, imitating some rude English tourists she had once had the misfortune to come across in Calais.

The teenager then pointed to the bottle of cider, but Aggie refused to acknowledge that she understood him.

"English," she said and then more firmly "English."

The teenagers gave up and wandered off with a gallic shrug of their shoulders.

"You handled that well," came the voice of a passing Englishman.

"Thank you. It is most bizarre to find French teenagers begging for alcohol. I would have expected it of English teenagers but not the French," said Aggie, as she took a second bite of her baguette.

"The problem is that there is a large group of them camped at the edge of the campsite. They are part of a project to give poor inner city children a holiday."

"Ahhh. That explains it. Thank you for telling me."

"My pleasure. Enjoy your meal."

"Thank you," replied Aggie and Miles in unison.

Lying in bed and trying to read her book, Miles disturbed Aggie's peace and quiet by engaging her in conversation.

"Who would you rather go out with? Benedict Cumberbatch or Martin Freeman?" enquired Miles.

"Neither," came the reply.

"How about Mark Gatiss?" tried Miles.

"No. Not my type," replied Aggie.

"How about Jeremy Irons?" persisted Miles.

"Far too old, darling."

"What about Robert Downey, Jr?" said Miles moving on to Marvel film actors.

"No not my type."

"How about Chris Hemsworth?"

"Darling, he is far too young for me," said Aggie hoping this would put an end to the questioning.

It didn't.

"How about Samuel L Jackson?" came Miles' next question moving up the age scale.

"No."

"What about Scarlett Johannson?" asked Miles realising that his mother was becoming more distracted by her novel than his line of questioning.

"Darling! I am not that way inclined and I don't think Scarlett Johannson is either," answered Aggie hoping that there was no one listening outside the tent to their conversation.

"How about Graham Norton?" enquired Miles moving from Marvel actors to the celebrated chat show host.

"He's lovely darling, but I doubt I am his type."

"Well, how about Macron – I am sure he appreciates women of a good vintage," replied Miles, turning his attention to French politics. To which there was no other option but to throw her pillow at him in the hope of shutting him up.

Aggie's phone then rang before Miles could come up with any more names. Just typical, she thought. She was nice and comfortable in her bed and Miles was starting to settle. Aggie picked up her phone and saw it was Doug calling her. With a sinking heart she pressed answer.

"Hang on," she said, without waiting for Doug to say anything.

Clambering out of her sleeping bag, she unzipped the sleeping compartment and kept her head low so as not to brush it against the roof of the tent. She didn't want to disturb Miles, so, she pulled on a skirt over her pyjama bottoms and clambered out of the tent and got into the passenger seat of her car.

"What's up?" she said.

"What were you doing?" came Doug's reply.

"I was in bed and have just got out of the tent and now I am in the car. How are you and how was your day?"

"Marvellous!" Oh God, thought Aggie as he started to bang on about his perfect holiday and perfect children.

"… and then there was an emergency at work, so, I have spent the last three hours trying to sort that out," continued Doug unhappily.

"Why can't they get someone else to do it? Your boss is there. Why can't he sort it out?"

"He is an idiot! You know that. It was so much better at my last company. We never had problems like this. The chain of command worked perfectly. Promoting idiots never works. They should be sacked."

"Why don't you start looking for another job?" suggested Aggie, suspecting she knew the answer.

"There won't be anything suitable for me locally and I have the children to think of," came the predictable reply. This conversation was a repeat of many they had had over the past six months. It was getting tiresome for Aggie.

"They are at a private school. At the worst they could board if your ex doesn't want them," suggested Aggie.

"Don't be ridiculous!" Then feeling the need to change the subject away from any criticism of the way he chose to lead his life. "How are you managing financially on your trip?" Aggie felt the knife go in.

"Okay. I had to buy a new mattress today which I hadn't planned on. As long as I am careful we should manage to get back from this trip without a huge credit card bill."

"You really are going to have to get a proper job when you get back," came Doug's authoritarian reply. Aggie could feel the knife go in deeper.

"I have a career as an artist," replied Aggie, finding some courage.

"It's not really a proper career is it? Let's face it you aren't managing to keep on top of the bills."

"Doug, I am too tired to have this kind of conversation at the moment. I haven't asked you for any money and it is a proper career." Aggie ended the call without wishing him a good night. She didn't have to energy to explain for the umpteenth time how the creative industries worked and she doubted he would ever understand. That was the problem with dating an 'executive' with a salary and bonus scheme.

Aggie got out of the car and was accosted again by the French teenagers asking for 'alcool'.

"Va te faire foutre," she said making the most of her French swear words.

Aggie was becoming increasingly frustrated by people attempting to take advantage of her. Far too often they were successful and thought that having succeeded once they could continue. A case in point was Doug who used her as a sounding board and wasn't really interested in what she had to say. Another was a local gift shop that had taken her greetings cards on sale or return, sold them and then the owner was conveniently unavailable when she phoned or turned up to collect her cash. She knew she would have to threaten him with court action and even take the matter further but hated to be forced into a position of getting tough.

This trip was going to draw a line at which she would no longer put up with people taking her for a ride. She would be firm, however hard it was for her not to be nice.

Week 1 – Day 3 - Vannes

Aggie had spent the night tossing and turning. She had been cold and her feet had refused to warm up. Thick socks hadn't helped as her feet had been cold before putting them on when getting into bed. However hard she had tried, she had been unable to get them warm. It had been uncomfortable as she had tried various positions from foetal to tucking each foot in turn behind the knee of the other leg in a bid to defrost each one. By the morning, after numerous trips to the toilet in the night, Aggie's head felt as though it had been stuffed with cotton wool. She vowed to wear a jumper and jeans in bed the following night.

Heading for the 'sanitaire' block for a shower, Aggie wondered whether she should incorporate cold showers into her pilgrimage routine. There must be some advantage to taking them – unless those that did were masochists – she thought. Would having one leave her feeling invigorated and full of joie de vivre to get on with the day? Thankfully the campsite they were currently staying on had a fixed temperature control on the showers. Phew, thought Aggie. A reprieve.

Sitting having her breakfast and taking in the early fresh morning air, Aggie began to reflect on her lack of finances and her attempts to rectify this major problem.

Fed up with pressure from Doug to get a 'proper' job she had applied for a job share assistant manager post at a local clothes retailer. Doug had been all for her application too. In fact, he had found the position for her which had not gone down well. Yes, she desperately needed to earn some money now that her savings were almost depleted but she also had a son to look after. What she really needed was a boyfriend who supported her career as an artist and didn't undermine it by suggesting roles that bore no relation to the arts industry at all. She needed encouragement and someone who would not demand her time when she should be working.

Fellow artist, Magda, had been encouraging Aggie with her artistic practice and pointing her in the direction of arts technician jobs at local schools but Doug had found the assistant manager job first. He had even helped her to fill in the online application form. She had felt railroaded.

The first interview had had Aggie phoning Magda in tears. The job hadn't been a job share as advertised but a full 48 hours a week with no time off in the school holidays. The promised salary had been the minimum wage made up to £30,000 in commissions. This probably meant that it was unlikely that she would earn anywhere near that amount with the state the economy was in. Doug had been thrilled. He had then started talking about city breaks and wouldn't it be fun to do one a month? Aggie would rather go for a walk in the countryside or save the money. Besides, when did he think they could go on these city breaks when she would be working each weekend?

Magda had been far more supportive and sensible. There would be no way Aggie could continue with her art if she worked those hours and, even though Miles was 16, he still needed her to be there when he got back from school – even if it was just to make him a post school snack or be a sounding board for something that had happened at school. Living in a village he also needed ferrying to and from friends and what about Aggie's social life? That would go. When did Doug think he would be able to see her? He certainly didn't have a higher priority than her son – even if he thought he did. Magda had reminded Aggie, even though she didn't need reminding, that she needed to find time to do things for herself as well.

The second interview came and this time it was with the area manager. The pressure by Doug to attend the interview regardless of the downsides was too great for Aggie to fight against. There was also no way she was going to lie about going to the interview if she hadn't attended. Aggie abhorred lying. There was only one other option: fail the interview. With Magda's help they had put together an outfit guaranteed to put off any interviewer: brightly coloured floral pantaloon trousers were matched with a clashing spotty t-shirt with sweat stains under the armpits – a gem of a find from her student days that had been in a crumpled heap at the back of her wardrobe. Also lurking underneath the t-shirt they found a pair of ancient Jesus sandals that had last seen the light of day during her university years. The look was close to bag lady but Magda felt that more needed to be done. She then dragged Aggie into the kitchen and stained her hands and feet with old wet tea bags. Her hair was coiffed into the wild woman of Borneo look and bright red lipstick was added as the finishing touch. The effect was 'hooker fallen on hard times.'

With a large vodka coursing through her veins, Aggie had walked into the store with her head held high. The first person she saw was one of the assistants ironing a dress.

"Marvellous!" Aggie said greeting the assistant. "I am so looking forward to working somewhere where I can do my ironing!"

The assistant laughed with embarrassment and introductions were made. On hearing Aggie's arrival, the area manager came over and took her to the interview room. He was visibly shocked by her appearance and struggled to compose himself before launching into the interview.

Aggie had been torn between demonstrating that she could do the job and making sure she wasn't offered it. She decided to let her appearance speak for itself and the interview lasted barely ten minutes. The area manager's frosty manner did nothing to reduce the stifling atmosphere in the room and Aggie really did not cope with high humidity. Sweat was running down her back and rivulets were turning into streams down her cleavage. As she was lead out of the room she came face to face with the next candidate. Icing needed to be added to the cake, thought Aggie, and addressed the appropriately attired man in a conventional suit.

"You look hot in that!" She was recovering her naughty side. "You would feel much cooler dressed like me!"

The man was too shocked to reply and Aggie walked out of the store as she had come in: head held high and vodka coursing through her veins. Aggie cringed at the memory as this behaviour was not like her at all. She suspected it had had something to do with the vodka.

After Miles had had his breakfast but was still in the teenage fug of not being fully awake even though he had eaten, they drove into Vannes and found a little side street near the port to park the car. It was going to be a 15 minute walk to the bottom of the town. Aggie desperately needed the exercise and to keep costs down. Miles was not impressed by the extra walking inflicted on him by his mother all in a bid to save money on parking.

It was a pleasant stroll alongside the marina. Aggie loved the sound of the ropes clanging on the masts of the sailing boats. Her mind wandered to thoughts of sailing around the coast of France and pulling into lovely ports like Saint Valery sur Somme, Honfleur, Saint Malo and Vannes. It was a shame she didn't have the money or the skill to sail. At least she was here and she could dream.

Her mind wandered to internet dating and she wondered if she could find a man who had his own boat. Her mind was now focused on creating the right profile picture that would attract such a man. She would need some photos of her wearing a stripy Breton top standing near some yachts. The fact that she still had a boyfriend hadn't escaped her attention. However, she was mentally preparing for the time when she would be single again.

Approaching the busy road in front of Porte Saint Vincent, Miles grabbed Aggie's arm to make sure she didn't walk in front of a car. She really was getting bad at road safety, thought Miles. He hoped she wasn't going senile. She wasn't. Her mind was still working on improving her internet dating profile pictures.

"Sorry, darling," said Aggie. "Now that you are older and not liable to walk in front of traffic I feel I can relax."

"Do you want to get yourself killed?" came Miles' sharp reply.

"Darling, I am quite safe. I won't get run over." Miles was not enjoying his new role as parent.

They walked through Porte Saint Vincent and headed up the hill and through the market. If only Aggie had dragged Miles out of bed earlier they wouldn't have had to battle their way through the crowds. Aggie's eye caught sight of a stall selling Breton tops and she mulled over whether her budget would stretch to one for her dating profile picture. It would be an improvement on one of her tie-dye t-shirts.

Before she had a chance to move in the direction of the stall, Miles pulled off his headphones and pointed out a man at one of the market stalls tasting some of the cheese.

"Oh look! There's Benedict Cumberbach," said Miles with enthusiasm.

"No it's not! It's a lookalike," came Aggie's reply.

"Yes it is!" persisted Miles. "Dare you to go up and ask for his autograph! Dare, dare and double dare!" said Miles re-enacting past holidays when he and Richard had dared each other to go up to random strangers and ask for their autographs.

"I am not feeling that brave," replied Aggie.

"Oh, you are so boring," harrumphed Miles putting his headphones back in place and marching at full speed through the shoppers and up the hill to the Eglise Saint Patern. Aggie hurried after him trying to combine a fast walk with a run and failing to look anything but ridiculous. At least Miles was ahead of her and couldn't see the spectacle she was making of herself.

Miles was now taller than Aggie. She was envious of his lovely long legs. Although she was regarded as tall at 5ft 7in, Aggie felt like a fat little pit pony compared to her friend Celia who, at 6ft in her heels, had all the attributes of a glamourous air hostess of times past. She wondered if Miles would end up taller than Celia. Both boys were blond and not dark like her and at first glance looked nothing like Aggie. Once, when the boys were toddlers, Aggie had been mistaken for their nanny. This had amused Betty who had responded to Aggie's telling of the tale with "who on earth would be mad enough to employ you as a nanny?" Both women had laughed. For they both knew Aggie was a good mother. However,

38

her unconventional approach to child management would put most parents off employing her as a nanny.

Anyone who looked closer at Miles or Richard would see the similarities in their facial features to Aggie. The almond eyes and the perfect lips were the same. Miles had a more masculine face than Aggie and an aquiline nose. His fine hair flopped over his forehead and somehow always looked neat even though he didn't possess a brush or a comb. Little did Aggie know that he regularly borrowed hers.

Walking into Eglise Saint Pattern, Aggie was taken by the calm atmosphere. She stood still and surveyed the church interior and took a deep breath before she started to walk around the church. This was the first of the seven stops on her pilgrimage and she hoped that, over the course of her journey, she would find some answers. One of the major stumbling blocks was that she didn't know the question. She just wanted to move on with her life.

It had been a good number of years since Aggie had regularly attended church. This, in part, had been due to the boys no longer wanting to attend and also her fear of going on her own. Doug would never go with her and had no spiritual leanings. It felt strange being back in a house of God again. It also felt welcoming.

She found a pew and sat down to pray. Meanwhile, Miles had placed himself down in one of the pews by the entrance and was busy listening to The White Stripes and was praying his bloody mother would hurry up. He was hungry.

Walking out of the church into the street, Aggie and Miles stopped and look at the medieval buildings facing the church.

"Let's go and get a Kouign Amann and a coffee," said Aggie. Her mouth was watering as she remembered the Breton pastries.

"Great idea. Can we go to that nice chocolate shop we passed on the way up and can I have one of their chocolates?" came the reply.

"Of course you can," replied Aggie feeling generous.

Weaving through the medieval streets towards the café at the bottom of the town, Aggie and Miles came across a gallery with a vibrant exhibition of large canvases depicting the Breton landscape.

Aggie grabbed Miles' arm to attract his attention and they headed into the gallery. Aggie was captivated by the artist's use of colour. She stood in front of one of the large canvases and became lost in the landscape. The use of colour was reminiscent of some of Hockney's work but yet again they were different and refreshing to Aggie's jaded eyes.

For the first time in years Aggie was feeling the first stirrings of desire to get back into creating new art. This exhibition of work by Jean Duquoc was so unlike anything she had seen in recent years in Kent. Even Miles was absorbed by the paintings.

Aggie approached the gallery assistant and asked about the works and prices. Even though she was wearing a tatty pair of jeans and loose crushed linen top the assistant took her enquiry seriously. The prices were way beyond anything she could normally afford but she didn't let on. She was enjoying pretending that she had the money and just needed to measure up the bare wall she had at home to see which one would fit. The lack of snootiness by the gallery staff was something Aggie found absent in UK gallery staff.

Before leaving, Aggie bought a selection of cards of her favourite paintings in the exhibition. She couldn't wait to tell Sally and Magda about the art she had discovered.

A little further down the hill they found another gallery. Miles was even more interested in this exhibition of rather strange nudes and started to surreptitiously take photos with his phone so he could send them via WhatsApp to his friends. Aggie glanced over at her son, raised her eyebrows and moved away. It was at times like this that Aggie felt it was better to pretend that Miles was not her son.

This exhibition didn't interest her as much as the landscapes and she only spent five minutes making a cursory look at each painting before walking out of the gallery and standing a short distance away from it. Getting her mobile phone out of her handbag she composed a text to Miles.

> Aggie - When you have finished photographing boobies, I am outside.

Inside Miles' phone beeped and he read the text and left the gallery and joined Aggie and gave her a cheeky smile. Aggie laughed and they walked on down the hill laughing at the pictures they had seen.

Aggie and Miles found the little café in Rue Saint Vincent to be relatively free of customers and chose a small table inside and sat down.

"Je suis fatigué," said Aggie after having placed their order. She could really do with an afternoon nap.

"I know you are fat and gay," came Miles' reply.

"Thank you, darling. You are so lucky you have me as your mother. Most parents would have grounded you for a week for saying such a thing." Miles laughed.

Aggie enjoyed spending time with her sons. The fact that they were a chip off the old block hadn't gone unnoticed. She was also acutely aware that Miles would soon be following Richard in flying the nest. She wanted to make the most of her time with him. Thoughts of Richard reminded her that he was home alone and she had better check up on him.

Aggie – Hello darling. How are things at home?

Richard – Good thanks. You have just woken me up!

Aggie – Did you have a late night last night?

Richard – Yeah.

Aggie – Hungover?

Richard – Yeah.

Aggie – Are the chickens and ducks okay?

Richard – Yeah. Magda has been coming over to sort them out.

Aggie – So, you haven't been looking after them at all?

Richard – Nope. Magda was worried they might die or be killed if left to me.

Aggie – You lazy sod!

Richard – My pleasure! Got to go. I feel sick.

Aggie – Don't be sick on the carpet!

Richard – Nope.

Aggie made a mental note to send a text to Magda later and thank her. Putting her phone away, she turned to Miles and asked after his cake.

After a light lunch, Aggie enjoyed her afternoon cup of tea outside the tent while eating a 'petit gateau' while Miles lay on his bed watching YouTube videos. The campsite was relatively quiet as most happy campers were off doing touristy things. She heard a beep in her handbag and got out her mobile phone. It was a text from Celia.

Celia – Finally got a date with Philip the accountant.

Aggie – Brilliant! That is about time. Why has it taken so long?

Celia – I didn't ask. I did check again on his height. He assures me he is 6ft 1in.

Aggie – That's good. So, at least he will be taller than you. That will make a change.

Celia – Such a relief! Unless he is lying!

Aggie – Did you check his age too????

Celia – No. He sounds young.

Aggie – Perhaps he has lied about his age the other way?

Celia – I hope not! I want to date someone the same age as me so I don't have to explain who the Bay City Rollers were.

Aggie – Or Adam and the Ants!

Celia – Don't mention Adam. My knees have already gone weak with the mention of the BCR's.

Aggie – So, when is the date?

Celia – Tomorrow. We are meeting at that café in West Malling.

Aggie – I want the low down as soon as you have said "goodbye" to him.

Celia was 5ft 10in without her much loved high heeled shoes. She resolutely refused to wear flat shoes and hated being seen out with a man shorter than herself as this caused her to stoop to match his height. She was always stylishly turned out – the polar opposite to Aggie's holiday or studio style. Even in her smart clothes, Aggie couldn't match Celia's style on a night out.

As Miles was still busy watching YouTube videos, Aggie seized the opportunity to catch up with Magda.

Aggie – Thank you so much for taking on the care of the chickens and ducks.

Magda – No problem. I thought they might not survive Richard's tender loving care and I think Betty has been eying them up for the pot.

Aggie – I bet she has! You are a true star. Richard said he would be able to look after them. He is in the dog house. Anyway, how's it going with you and how is work?

Magda – All good here. Just got another commission. It is a bloody pet portrait though!

Aggie – Couldn't you turn it down?

Magda – No, I need the money. I have told them I will only do it in pastels and my usual style. They wanted me to Disney-fy it! I did say that if that was what they wanted I probably wasn't the right artist for them. They still wanted me to do it and at £300!

Aggie – Why didn't you say you would Disney-fy it for £500?

Magda – That would be like prostitution! No way! It is my style or not at all. After that portrait I did last year where they kept changing their minds on the style – it worked out at £1 an hour for my time.

Aggie – Well done on sticking to your principles.

Magda – Merci! How goes it in France?

Aggie – Still ruminating on Doug. He keeps telling me that I would love it down there. I can't stand his children and he doesn't listen to me. He is also continuing to pressurise me to get a 'proper' job.

Magda – You keep telling me you want to dump him.

Aggie – I know and I am going to do it this holiday. I am going to do it this week. I am just going through that yucky stage of knowing the deed has to be done and actually doing it.

Magda – You need to clear out thoughts of Doug from your head. Get rid of all that rubbish. This will leave room for all the good things in the universe to rush in and fill that void.

Aggie – I know! Making that first step is always the hardest thing.

Magda – Start off by trying not to think about him – make a little space in your head first of all.

Aggie – Thanks. I will try.

Magda – You are one of the bravest people I know. You are more than capable of dumping him and picking yourself up off the floor, dusting yourself down and getting on with your life.

Aggie – Thanks. I will do it. I promise. I just need to mentally prepare myself for the phone call.

Magda – Go for it and let me know when you are a free woman!

Aggie – Will do! Good luck with the pet portrait.

Aggie put her phone down and sat back and looked at Miles through the tent opening. He was still immersed in a YouTube video.

"Fancy a game of cards?" she asked.

"Nah," came the reply.

Miles stopped watching his video and started to tap into his 'notes' app on his phone. He then converted it to text to speech. It was a quote from The Italian Job.

"You are only supposed to blow the bloody door off." Hearing such an iconic phrase spoken in such a stilted manner made Aggie laugh.

"You do one," said Miles, handing the phone to her.

Aggie tapped away, looking up at Miles' face from time to time and giving him a mysterious smile. When she had finished typing she looked up, raised her eyebrows and winked at him.

"Say 'hello' to my little friend," came the stilted voice of the phone. They both giggled like 12-year-olds. Aggie handed the phone back to Miles who gave her a cheeky grin and started tapping into the 'notes' app. They continued the game until it was time to go and buy supper. Before they knew it, it was time for bed. Aggie was shattered and glad of a chance to lie down.

Aggie lay in bed thinking how nice it was to relax at the end of the day. In recent years, she had spent many evenings catching up on her painting until two in the morning. That was one of the advantages of being an artist. It was flexible enough to fit around her parenting duties. It was also the downside as she never had a chance to relax at home.

Week 1 – day 4 - Vannes

It hadn't been until midnight that it had started to dawn on Aggie that sleeping on an airbed was making the cold and damp creep into her body. She needed to have something between her sleeping bag and the airbed. A single duvet might help and would be useful when she got home. She hated spending yet more money, however, she would have to buy it in order to ensure she slept well while they were camping.

At 3 am the storm that was raging overhead increased it's ferocity. Aggie woke and lay listening to the heavy downpour as it ricochet off her tent and watched, in the dim light, as the roof of the tent was buffeted and pummelled. Aggie could hear what sounded like a stream outside the tent. She could feel the need to go to the toilet, yet again, but was trying to delay the inevitable when one of the guy ropes came loose.

There was nothing for it but to wake Miles and ask for his help. It was a seriously grumpy Miles that greeted her request for assistance. Surely she could manage on her own he had asked? No, she couldn't. Then another guy rope pinged and the back of the tent started to cave in over the sleeping compartment.

They both hauled on their macs and clambered out of the tent. The wind and rain buffeted them and their feet sank into the wet, soggy, rain filled grass outside their tent. They each grabbed a guy rope and pulled it taut and attached it to the corresponding tent peg. Ping! Another guy rope had freed itself from its mooring. Aggie ran around to grab the rope as it flailed around in the wind and rain. Miles held onto the tent to stop it from moving so that it didn't dislodge any more guy ropes.

Aggie dived into the tent and grabbed some more pegs and they both started to peg out the spare guy ropes that were loosely hanging on the tent. Aggie didn't believe in pegging out all of the tent when putting it up. It had seemed like overkill when they had first set up the tent. She was beginning to regret this sentiment as they struggled to peg down more ropes.

By the time they crawled back into the tent they were drenched. Miles dumped his wet mac on the floor of the tent and started to dry his legs and face with his towel. Aggie was just about to do the same when her bladder reminded her that the reason she woke up in the first place was to go to the toilet. The wind and the rain had increased the urgency.

"Shit," she said. "I need a pee." With that she took a deep breath and unzipped the tent and stepped outside.

Arriving back at the tent, she saw a rip near where one of the guy ropes joined the tent. She then made an inspection of the rest of the tent and saw other smaller tears. This was the problem with buying a budget tent, she thought to herself. There was no way the tent would survive the rest of the holiday. They would have to buy another one. This was all she needed – yet more expense. She crawled back into her sleeping bag and fell into a deep sleep.

Waking early, Aggie got up and clambered out of the sleeping compartment and found some dry jeans and a thick dry jumper and headed off to the toilet block.

Returning to the tent, and without disturbing Miles, Aggie then settled down to her early morning coffee and a supermarket pain au chocolate. Opening the plastic packaging, she removed one of the pastries and took a deep breath, savouring the moment and

Journey by Liz Garnett

anticipating the deep joy of sinking her teeth into a sweet and full butter pastry. It took one bite for Aggie to realise she had made a mistake. The pain au chocolate didn't taste very nice at all. Where was the buttery flavour she had been expecting? She picked up the packaging and looked at it in more detail. Then she saw that they had been made with 'tournesol'. Sunflower oil. Oh why hadn't she read the packaging? Then she thought, this is Brittainy, land of butter. That was her morning ruined.

Packing up the ripped, wet tent was a relatively easy task. Aggie and Miles salvaged the poles, rope and pegs and then Miles carted the rest of it to the 'poubelles' and dumped it in one of the large refuse bins. Trying to squeeze a tent into it's bag was always difficult for Aggie and a wet one would have been a nightmare. It would have been a battle of wills to do up the zip. So, she was somewhat relieved to not be carting it with them.

Once they were in the car, Aggie set the sat nav to find the nearest Decathlon, which wasn't far. They set off, leaving the campsite and village outside Vannes behind them. Aggie felt apprehensive about going even further from home. Part of her hated being too far away from Richard in case there was an emergency. Miles was also apprehensive about being further away from his brother. He was missing him and the daft holiday games they played. His mind was working out whether he could persuade his mother to play a burping game that had been great fun on past holidays. He suspected not.

Decathlon was easy to find and only a short hop from Leclerc on the opposite side of the autoroute to Carrefour. Aggie was excited at the thought of trying out another supermarket. Miles was equally thrilled and wondered what goodies he would find there.

Aggie made a quick and, she hoped, wise choice of tent in Decathlon and then they both dived into Leclerc in search of more bedding and a picnic lunch. Miles headed straight for the sweets and biscuits in a bid to make sure these weren't forgotten.

Having selected a suitable duvet to insulate her airbed against the cold and damp, Aggie went in search of food for a picnic. The supermarket baguettes weren't as nice as the ones from a boulangerie, but they would have to do. She then went in search of some stinky French cheese. She fancied some Langres cheese but could only track down a Petit Pont l'Eveque from Normandy. To this she added some tomatoes and olives as a nod to two of their five a day.

Miles came and found her as she was just leaving the fruit and veg section. His arms were laden with paprika crisps, Orson mini cakes, Haribo Schtroumpfs and a bottle of grenadine syrop. Aggie was tired and in no mood to question the wisdom of his choice.

At the tills Aggie let Miles key in the pin number to her credit card. This didn't go unnoticed and the checkout girl, who was in her thirties, remarked on the bravery of Aggie in letting her son know her pin number. She said she hoped Miles would take her out to lunch. Aggie, knowing that Miles would understand the French, said to him that he had pulled to which the checkout girl responded by saying that she was too old for him. Both women laughed and Miles buried his head in his phone in embarrassment.

As they drove towards Quimper the weather continued to be grey with intermittent showers mirroring Aggie and Miles' mood. When they reach Quimperlé they pulled into a parking space at Place Charles de Gaulle overlooking the river Laïta and got out their picnic. They enjoyed baguette stuffed with cheese and looked out of the window at the passing scene. Miles then tucked into his 'pudding' of blue Harribo Schtroumpfs and stuck his blue tongue out at Aggie.

"That is quite revolting, darling," said Aggie.

"But yummy! Would you like a smurf?"

"No thanks!" came Aggie's reply, remembering a holiday many moons before in which Miles had gorged himself on the blue Harribo sweets and ended up covered in a blue sticky mess. The car hadn't fared much better either.

As the rain beat down on the windscreen for the umpteenth time, Aggie reminded Miles of the time they had been in Rouen and had had to buy umbrellas. The boys had been 10 and 12 years old and, when the rain had stopped, had used the umbrellas as weapons of war. Miles would have liked to have an umbrella duel with his mother but recognised that she was not a worthy opponent.

Lunch completed, Aggie and Miles drove up and out of Quimperlé. Aggie had been too tired for a walk around the town and they enjoyed a companionable silence as they drove through the scenic and green Finisterre countryside to Quimper. They passed through small villages and Aggie tried to absorb the changes in the architecture of the buildings as they passed through but it was a battle to overcome her tiredness.

At one point, as they drove through the rural landscape, they slowed down to overtake a parked car and both giggled as they saw the driver standing in the bushes, back to the road, having a pee. Only in France, they said to each other, enjoying the cultural differences between France and the UK.

The journey gave Aggie the chance to reflect on her current situation. Increasingly, she had felt as though she was walking through treacle. She knew the direction she wanted to go yet obstacles had been thrown in her path. Being tired didn't help matters. Aggie continued to reflect on the impasse in her art and dwelt on the misery of dating Doug. Back in Kent, each day felt as if it was a repeat of the day before.

Finding the Quimper campsite couldn't have been easier. It was just off the main road. Unfortunately, as Aggie got out of the car and headed to the reception, the heavens opened. This was all she needed. However, luck was on her side as signing-in was easy and the map of the campsite with their 'emplacement' highlighted was simple to understand. Within 10 minutes of arriving at the site they were on their pitch trying to decide how to pitch the tent while the heavens emptied as much water on them as possible.

It was at times like these that Miles came into his own and his ability to understand written instructions was thanks to years of creating Lego models. Aggie rarely followed instructions and was grateful for his help. She wondered what Doug was doing and what he would have made of their trip if he had come with them. Aggie smiled to herself as she thought about how much he would have hated the experience. He would have turned his nose up at their picnic meals and one pot suppers. Ultimately, he would not have understood why she needed to do a pilgrimage. He preferred to wallow in self-pity while Aggie wanted to seek solutions.

Once they had set up their new tent in the rain, Aggie and Miles went in search of the campsite bar to get warm and dry off. The bar was full of families sitting around tables glued to their tablets and smartphones. This saddened Aggie as she enjoyed spending time with her sons and particularly liked playing a game of Risk with

Miles on his smartphone. They chose a table and Miles sat down while Aggie went to the bar and ordered drinks. When she got back to the table Miles had set up a game of Risk and they spent the next hour and a half happily immersed in the game while chatting about this and that and drying out.

Leaving the bar, Miles plugged his headphones back into his ears leaving Aggie to her thoughts of life after Doug. She was thinking like this and she hadn't even finished with him. It was inevitable that she would and sooner rather than later. She was dreading that phone call. It did seem a bit mean to do it over the phone and not in person. However, she couldn't mentally move on until she had dumped him and it would be five weeks before they were next due to see each other. He was due to go away on business shortly after she returned from her holiday and he had specifically said that there was no way he would have time to meet up with her before he went away. His enthusiasm for seeing her had also waned over the last few months. It had had to be on his terms and she had been expected to drop everything at a moment's notice.

How on earth had she got herself into this mess? This was a question she couldn't answer. Or was it that she didn't want to answer it. There was only one thing to do and that was to phone him before the week was out. Dump him. Be firm. Then she could move on. Hopefully, inspiration would start to flow once the deed had been done.

The sun was finally shining brightly by the time they got back to their tent and Aggie gathered together their dirty laundry and headed to the 'laverie'. Aggie found the simple tasks of living helped her to gain a perspective on her everyday life back in Kent. Simple camping holidays focussed on the everyday experience of existing: finding food, cooking, washing-up and laundry. Walking into the laundry room, Aggie found the building empty and all the machines vacant. She loaded a machine with their dirty clothes and grudgingly paid the extortionate fee for the wash. They would have to wear their clothes for more than one day, she decided. She was certain that the campsite 'laveries' were more expensive than the ones in town but didn't want to go to the trouble of driving into town to do the washing. She then sat down cross legged on an uncomfortable plastic chair and started to meditate. To solve the problem of how to move forward with her life she was throwing everything she could at it.

At 10 pm her phone rang just as she was about to turn her light off. She had failed to get anywhere with reading her book because musings on Doug were getting in the way of her wind down reading time. Ugghh! It was Doug. She answered it with a heavy heart.

"Hello. Hang on a minute and I will get out of bed and take this call in the car," she said.

Aggie clambered out of the sleeping compartment of the tent and pulled on her skirt and then emerged from the tent and slipped on her flip flops.

Unlocking the car she got in, closed the door quietly and then spoke.

"Sorry." Why was she apologising? "I didn't want to disturb Miles. How are you?"

"Wonderful! We have had a great day. You would love it down here," replied Doug full of enthusiasm for his holiday.

"As I said before, it would have been too far for me to drive." Came Aggies heavy reply reflecting on all the rain they had had that day.

"You could have flown," replied Doug, undeterred by Aggie's tone.

"I don't like flying."

"You can take pills for that." He really didn't get it, thought Aggie.

"We went sailing today – it was great! Not a cloud in the sky," continued Doug. Aggie raised her eyes heavenward. This guy really was not getting the message, thought Aggie.

 "How are the girls getting on?"

"Oh, they have been bickering all day long." Still Doug seemed not to be phased by this. So, not that great thought Aggie.

"So, they didn't enjoy the sailing?"

"Oh, I am sure they did," replied Doug. Aggie wondered if Doug had any grip on the reality of the behaviour and thoughts of his daughters.

Aggie thought about the day she had had with Miles, while Doug prattled on about the marvels of the South of France. Aggie's holiday couldn't have been more different. Today the weather had been grey and wet and now all they had to look forward to was a night in a cold and damp tent. She still didn't want to be in the South of France with Doug and his frightful daughters. She enjoyed Miles' company and she had had fun speaking French. Any trip with Doug would have reduced the opportunities for her to practice her French. Being with him meant she missed opportunities for interesting conversations with strangers and speaking French meant she got to exercise her brain.

"... oh and our meal out tonight was out of this world! It was 75 euros a head but well worth it!" continued Doug, oblivious of Aggie's lack of attention.

"I am sorry, Doug, I am going to have to go," was Aggie's response as she thought about her supper. A one pot vegetable stew with fresh baguette and lashings of delicious Breton butter. Simple, cheap and full of flavour.

Cutting the call. Aggie got out of the car, locked it and unzipped the tent.

Snuggling deep into her sleeping bag she reflected on Doug's phone call. Not once had he asked about her day. Aggie was horrified at the cost of the meal – 75 euros a head. She then thought about the cost of their meals and realised it would be around 75 euros a week for both of them. Doug had really been rubbing salt into her wounds. He knew she was struggling financially. The thing was, she thought, she wasn't jealous of the meal Doug had had. It was just his lack of consideration. He liked her paintings but never bought any as he expected to be given them as presents. When she had had private views and suggested he invite some of his friends and colleagues he had refused. To Aggie there was some kudos in being invited to a private view. To Doug it was nothing of the sort.

Week 1 – day 5 – Quimper

Aggie awoke at 6.30 am. Bliss. She had had a decent night's sleep thanks to the addition of the new bedding. She scrambled out of the sleeping compartment and pulled on her skirt over her pyjamas and headed for the toilet block. She was desperate for a pee and didn't want to check her phone otherwise she would be distracted with any texts from Celia that had come in during the night. At last, it looked like it might be a sunny day.

Once Aggie had settled herself in front of her little gas stove with the pan of water on its way to boil, she checked her phone. No text from Celia. So she sent one, knowing it was too early for Celia to reply but she could expect a reply once Celia was awake.

> Aggie – So, how did it go? Was Phillip all that he claimed to be? I stayed up as long as I could waiting for a text from you last night.

Celia's reply came in just as Aggie was biting into her all butter supermarket croissant.

> Celia – Too awful for words. Sorry, I didn't call. I drove home in floods of tears.

> Aggie – Why?

> Celia – Firstly, he was shorter than me and secondly he kept trying to hold my hand. His hand was damp and clammy!

> Aggie – Yuk! I think, henceforth, I shall call him Fumbling Phil.

Celia – There is going to be no 'henceforth'! When I said goodbye to him I had to have the car door between me and him so that he couldn't lunge at me with a wet, slobbery kiss.

Aggie – LOL! You do make me laugh!

Celia – I don't understand why he would be so stupid as to think I wouldn't notice his height.

Aggie – Are you sure he was an accountant? He is clearly not good with numbers!

Celia – Yes he is and he was as predictably boring as everyone imagines them to be!

Aggie – There must be some who aren't.

Celia – You can't begin to imagine how boring this one was!

Aggie – Anyway, why are you up this early?

Celia – I couldn't sleep. I was too depressed to sleep. I have also used it as an opportunity to rejig my dating profile to make me sound more interesting.

Aggie – Really sorry to hear you are down. At least re-jigging your profile is a positive step. Have you added that you want a man with a hairy chest?

Celia – No! Tempting but no. I look at the photos for clues to a hairy chest!

Aggie – LOL! Some of them are helpful by adding photos of them at the pool but all the ones I have seen seem to be free of chest hair.

Celia – I know! One chap had his t-shirt pulled up to display his fine rotund belly!

Aggie – Seriously? Not sexy! I always try to hide my worst features in my profile pictures which is getting harder and harder the older I get.

Celia – I know, right! Getting the right angle to hide the double chin or wearing long sleeved tops to hide the bat wings.

Aggie - LOL! Has your work thrown up any interesting contacts?

Celia – I have a new client so that is a positive.

Aggie – That's great! Good luck with that. I had better go and let you get some more sleep.

Celia – Catch you later.

Celia worked as a business consultant specialising in improving the finances of small or sole trader businesses. Celia and Aggie had met at an indoor soft play area when their children were pre-schoolers. They had both joined their children on the equipment and Aggie had helped Celia extricate herself from one of the tunnels.

Once Miles had unearthed himself from his sleeping bag, they set off for Quimper. Aggie drove confidently into the town centre.

Having the sat nav made getting into and out of towns easier than just following the signs blindly in the hope that she was going in the right direction. It wasn't until Aggie had crossed the River Odet that ran through and to the east of the main town that she realised she might have difficulty in parking. Shit, she thought to herself. Where was she going to park? Every available street parking space was full and there was nowhere to 'create' a parking space. Miles was no help as he was plugged into the music on his phone and busy looking through the photos he had taken in Vannes.

Focussing on looking for 'P' for parking signs took them up a street to the other side of the main shopping area where she eventually found a large car park. However, within minutes she realised it was full to bursting. Aggie then spied some creative parking by local drivers and decided to follow suit. This was what she loved about France. If there wasn't a parking space but room to 'create' one, it was done. No hassle. Aggie found a space on a verge next to a local car and manoeuvred her car into the space. Phew. She had found the experience more stressful than she had expected. Closing her eyes for a few minutes, she collected her thoughts before pulling the key out of the ignition and getting out of the car.

"Café, first stop, I think," she said to Miles.

A grunt was all she got in response as Miles got out of the car while still engrossed in his phone.

Miles and Aggie then wove their way to Place Saint Corentin which was overlooked by the cathedral and thronged by tourists and locals buying from the busy market.

Once installed at an outside café table bordering the Place, Miles switch his attention away from his phone and onto the scene around him and in particular his mother. Now that he was fully awake, he decided to engage in a conversation with Aggie.

"Mother, who would you rather date? Boris Johnson or Michael Gove?"

Aggie raised her eyebrows and looked at her son.

"Is that the best you can do?" she asked.

Feeling that this line of conversation was getting nowhere, Miles looked around the café for inspiration. Ahh, he thought, seeing a familiar face at a nearby table.

"Oh look! There's Martin Clunes," he said to Aggie.

"Where?"

"Over there!" Miles pointed to a grey haired man with a moustache. "Martin Clunes. The actor who played Inspector Clouseau in the Pink Panther films."

"That's not Martin Clunes!" responded Aggie. "You are thinking of Steve Martin." They both laughed. "You are right he does look like Steve Martin as Inspector Clouseau and no I won't go and ask him for his autograph."

"Spoilsport!" retorted Miles.

"But I might be interested in dating Steve Martin," added Aggie to placate Miles with his dating enquiries. They looked at each other and laughed again.

Sitting in the café, they continued to watch the market and marvel at the way the locals greeted each other with a kiss on each cheek. The tourists stood out like sore thumbs as they moved around the Place and shouted loudly to their badly behaved offspring. Aggie and Miles giggled as they played 'guess the nationality' of different tourists.

After having been revived at the café, they headed across the Place to the cathedral. Standing in front of the cathedral dedicated to Saint Corentin, Aggie took in the ornate carvings around the entrance and let her eyes follow the building upwards to the statue of King Gradlon who had founded the town. Flanking the statue were two spires ornately carved in stone. She marvelled at the creativity in the design.

Aggie paused for a moment, collecting her thoughts before entering the building and mentally ticking off stage two of her pilgrimage.

Inside the cathedral the air was cool. Following her in, Miles wandered off to take more photos and explore the religious artworks. Aggie stood at the back of the building and looked around, taking in the vast structure of the cathedral and looking at how the light came in through the stained glass windows. She felt transported to another world as peace and calm washed over her. Looking around, she saw a map and guide to the cathedral. Picking one up and putting some money in a little tin, she opened up the leaflet.

With the leaflet guiding her, she walked slowly around the cathedral, anti-clockwise, looking at each chapel in turn until she reached the chapel of Saint Corentin. Here she stood and took in all the features of the chapel. Having taken in the stained glass window, Aggies eyes fell on the statue of Saint Corentin. She spent some minutes absorbing all the details of the statue before closing her eyes and praying. She prayed for hope and her friends and family.

Having finished his photography and exploration of the building, Miles spied Aggie praying and waited until she had opened her eyes before coming up behind her and putting his hands over her eyes and speaking in a French accent:

"Guess who ziss is?" Aggie laughed. Miles always knew how to make her laugh.

After lunch, Aggie and Miles changed into their swimwear and headed to the campsite pool. Miles was hoping that he could get away with not wearing speedos or, as his mother preferred to call them, 'budgie smugglers'. On past holidays, Richard and Miles had been told off by the lifeguard for wearing board shorts. Aggie was equally horrified by the no board shorts rule. She was a firm believer that some men should have more of their body covered up. She found seeing men with large bellies hanging over the top of tiny speedos was too horrific for words. Her Aunt Betty refused to wear prescription sun glasses in such circumstances – preferring to see as little as possible. Aggie reflected that it was fortunate not to have Betty on holiday with them as she was liable to make loud comments about obesity at such times. As Betty was also going deaf she was completely unaware that she could be heard making such comments. Women fared no better under her steely gaze. Aggie now refused to take her into town when the temperature went above 15°C for fear of Betty's remarks on the dress sense and lack of clothing of the local inhabitants. "Oh my God! What does she think she looks like!" was one of her favourite phrases along with, "Really! That skirt is more a belt than a skirt!" and "Is it really necessary to wear a crop top with such a large tummy?" On more than one occasion Aggie had had to point out that the woman in question was at least 8 months pregnant.

The sky was overcast and the air felt damp. It really wasn't warm enough, in Aggie's eyes, for swimming but it was a good way of entertaining Miles. She hoped her faded Speedo swimming costume would survive the holiday. There were definite patches of very thin material that could easily fail to resist the strain of her body. She was grateful for the reinforcement around the bust.

Walking into the fenced off pool area Miles took one look at the teenagers using the slide and declared that there was no way he would use the slide.

"Why?" enquired Aggie.

"Look at them!" He said, pointing at the boys at the top of the slide. "They're pulling up their 'budgie smugglers' between their bum cracks," he said in disgust. Both Aggie and Miles were mystified as to why the French teenagers were making this strange adjustment to their clothing, but concluded it must be to increase their speed going down the slide. Aggie pitied the skin on their poor bottoms which, she surmised, would be red raw after an afternoon on the waterslide.

"I think you need to go up there and show them how to dam up the top of the slide. Your French is good enough to tell them that you go faster that way and without your bottom hanging out."

Miles harrumphed and looked at his mother. He was missing Richard who would have led the way. There was really no option for him. On the one hand he could try and persuade his mother to join him in the pool or he could go up the slide and join these teenagers with strange habits. Then he had an idea.

"Mother dearest. Will you join me on the slide?"

Aggie groaned inwardly as it wasn't really warm enough for her to swim and there were no other adults in the pool.

"Pretty please?" Begged Miles.

"Oh, okay then," she replied, reluctantly. She really did need to have a swim and work on her fitness. Plunging into the pool via the slide might be just what she needed.

They headed up the slide and Miles offered to dam it up for her. Aggie had more sense. She wanted to go down the slide at a sedate pace. Just as she had settled herself at the top of the slide and was about to take a deep breath before launching herself down the slide, Miles gave her a big push. In his opinion, he felt she needed it to get up enough speed.

Aggie screamed as she hurtled down the slide and plunged into the freezing cold pool. Miles smiled. Brilliant. His mother had now woken any happy campers who were taking a post lunch nap. With his first mission accomplished and a group of assorted French and German teenagers behind him he proceeded to explain to them the best way to achieve maximum velocity down the slide. Thankfully, they were all shorter than him and didn't question his authority. With their help, he blocked the water from going down the slide, to build up a good body of water behind him, before launching himself down the curved, semi-tubular slide. As he went down, his body went first up one side and then the other. Aggie, watching from the pool had her heart in her mouth as she feared he might go so fast and then up and over the edge. Oh why had she suggested he dam up the slide?

Miles was swiftly followed, one by one, by the other teenagers. They were clearly enjoying his style of speeding down the slide and soon Miles was making friends and coming up with innovative ways of going down the slide. Aggie decided against watching as it was all too terrifying. A health and safety expert would have had kittens if he could have seen what was going on. Sticking to swimming methodically up and down the pool, Aggie concentrated on counting laps before getting out and wrapping a beach towel around her wet body.

An hour later, just as Miles was starting to get bored, the heavens opened. He ran over to where Aggie was sitting and grabbed his beach towel and they trotted back to the tent chatting happily about Miles' fun on the waterslide. Even though it had started to rain hard, their spirits had been lifted by the suddenness of the downpour and the need to head to shelter. The cold rain was invigorating.

After supper, while Aggie was sitting outside the tent trying to read her book, she decided that it was time to give Doug the boot. Miles was having a shower. Knowing him, he would be at least half an hour. She hoped that the other happy campers in the shower block didn't mind his singing. Thinking of him singing in the shower made her smile.

Aggie picked up her phone, unlocked the screen and pressed the phone symbol and then the little square with Doug's name on it. Uggghh she thought to herself, she wasn't looking forward to this call one little bit.

"Hello."

"Hello Doug, how was your day?" came Aggie's reply. Better start off nice and cheerfully.

"Great! We spent the day in Saint Tropez. You would have loved it!" came the reply. Clearly he wasn't getting the message that she didn't want to be reminded of something glorious that she was missing. Although, spending time with Doug and his awful children would not have been marvellous.

"Listen, Doug, I don't think this is working." She said plucking up the courage to start the dumping process.

"You mean us?" came his somewhat startled reply.

"Yes." Don't say too much she told herself.

"Have you met anyone else?"

"No." What was he on? When would she have the time to meet anyone else?

"Why? I thought we were a good match."

"Well, I don't. We have different ideas about life and our aspirations aren't compatible." No, no, no, no, no! What was she doing explaining herself? No explanations! Just get it over and done with!

"So, you haven't met anyone else, then?" he asked.

"No." Well done! Keep it short.

"Well, you are going to find it hard to find someone else."

"What do you mean?" said Aggie, starting to panic that he was going to draw it out. No, she was not going to change her mind.

"Well, at your age!" he said.

"Seriously?" Keep it short, Aggie told herself. Don't let him drag you into a discussion. At her age indeed! He was the same age as her.

"Yes, you are lucky to have me," came the reply. He had to be kidding!

"Really?" said Aggie trying to keep focussed on saying as little as possible in case she really let rip.

"Yes. Women at your age aren't of interest to men. You have started to lose your looks and your body is getting saggy," said Doug with all the confidence of a middle aged man with an expanding waistline who hadn't looked in the mirror since he was in his 20s.

"With that kind of attitude, I am even happier now to part ways with you. You don't deserve me," came Aggie's reply, having failed to pay attention to her inner dialogue but feeling relieved to have said it.

She hung up just as Miles was sauntering back to the tent.

"What did you sing?" asked Aggie.

"Stayin' Alive," came the reply.

"I do hope the other happy campers gave you a round of applause when you finished!"

"No, I think I managed to clear the shower block with the first two verses of the song." With that Miles dived into the tent and got into bed and plugged himself into his phone.

With a deep breath and tears streaming down her face Aggie locked herself in her car and phoned Celia.

"I'm so sorry to call," she said.

"What's up, hon?" came the reply.

"I have just dumped Doug. I feel like shit but I can't be at his beck and call at the drop of a hat," she said. "He banged on about how marvellous his bloody holiday is in the South of France and how I would love it. I am in a tiny tent. It is cold and keeps pouring with rain!"

"You did the right thing."

"I know! I just feel like shit."

"There is more to life than arseholes."

Laughing, Aggie replied: "Yes!"

With a big blow on a large piece of toilet roll she wiped her tears away.

"Thanks for that. Cheer me up with your dating tales."

"Well, I think that may have you even more depressed!" laughed Celia.

"If the latest was a disaster, you will have me howling with laughter as usual! So, tell all. How was David?" said Aggie starting to cheer up at the thought of a good giggle.

"Well that is the last time I meet a man at the village tea rooms! He stank!"

"No! Not like the chap you met there who hadn't bathed for two days on top of a weekend of non-stop jive dancing?"

"Yes! This one had clearly been gardening and was still in his polo top and shorts. Nil points for effort," sighed Celia.

"But was he nice? Did he have any redeeming features?"

"Well, he could talk and hold eye contact and did have me laughing but that might have been out of nervous embarrassment."

"What is it with these men?"

"I don't know. He was overweight too. When I said I had been ill he said he was the very picture of health. I didn't like to point out that he was a heart attack waiting to happen."

"I know! They get to a certain age and can't see their faults or their age and still expect to bag a woman who is slim and looks about twenty."

"Yes! Do you remember that teacher I met who gave me an 'appraisal' at the end of our first date and said I needed to dye my greying hair?"

"Yes! You should have told him they were very expensive grey highlights!"

" I never think of these things at the time. He was also very rude about my smart black jeans."

"Good heavens! You met in a pub! Did he expect you to wear a cocktail dress?"

"Probably! What an idiot! I think I am as bad as you on the dating front. Do you remember Simon?" responded Aggie.

"Was he the one who had a large house in Spain, large pile in Kent and a loft apartment in London?"

"Yes. I still haven't recovered from going out for a third date at a smart gastro pub and Simon turning up in shorts."

"It was the shoes and socks that got me," replied the horrified Celia.

"Yes, socks and shorts. What style! I can't get over his acceptance of my offer to pay half when I clearly didn't have much money."

"Well, from what I know of you and your dating, it is that when you offer to pay half you don't intend on seeing them again."

"No. I felt guilty as he was complaining about the cost of his divorce so I offered to pay half."

"If he had insisted on paying what would you have done?"

"Given him a brownie point and a second chance."

"Love it!" laughed Celia.

"So, how did the date end?" enquired Aggie.

"Don't ask! Anyway, I have a date with a very nice man that I met in the supermarket."

"Oh when? Do tell all."

"Not much to tell, except he is taller than me, good looking and we both like brussels sprouts!" said Celia with a mysterious note to her voice.

"Sounds exciting except for the sprouts business. You strange woman! Where are you meeting and when?"

"Next week in Canterbury. I will keep you posted. And on that note, I had better leave you and make hot chocolates for the children. Do you feel any better now?"

"Yes and thank you! You are such a good friend! Onwards and upwards!" replied Aggie. Both women now felt rejuvenated and Aggie felt able to survive the night in a damp tent while the forecasted storm raged overhead.

Before getting out of the car Aggie sent a quick text to Magda with the update.

> Aggie – Done the deed!
>
> Magda – Well done! Now go to bed and get some sleep!
>
> Aggie – Yes Ma'am! You sleep well too!

Getting back into the tent and manoeuvring herself into her sleeping bag, Miles, poked his head out of his cocoon.

"Everything okay?"

"Yes, darling. I have just split up with Doug," replied Aggie feeling it was important to be honest with Miles.

"Sorry that you are sad but he was a real dickhead," was all that Miles could think of to say. Inside his sleeping bag he silently rejoiced.

"Darling, that is a little harsh." Was that really what Miles thought of him?

"Mum, he didn't think of you, he was up himself and never spoke to us. What do you want me to say?"

"Fair point. Now go back to sleep."

Aggie tried to get off to sleep but failed miserably. She lay in bed thinking about Doug and what he had said. His words raged around her head like a whirling dervish despite her attempts to banish them. By 11 pm the wind had increased and she could hear the first tentative drops of rain. Then, within 15 minutes the heavens had opened and the gusts of wind were buffeting the tent. Aggie's eyes opened and she watched the roof of the inner tent as it rocked from side to side. After ten minutes, with no let up, Aggie hauled herself out of bed and pulled on her skirt over her pyjamas and crawled out of the tent. There was just enough light from the campsite lighting for her to find her way around the tent and add new tent pegs and peg down the spare guy ropes. She still hadn't learnt the lesson to peg out all the guy ropes when setting up. Oh well, she thought, that brief interlude had taken her mind off Doug. She wondered how he was feeling. Was he missing her? She doubted it.

Journey by Liz Garnett

Week 1 – day 6 – Quimper

Aggie woke at 6 am to the sound of birdsong and something unidentifiable. She tried to listen harder and block out the birdsong in order to pinpoint the strange noise. What was it that she could hear? It couldn't be could it? Oh no. It was. Yes, she was sure it was definitely a couple having sex. That was all she needed. Couldn't they have been quieter, she wondered as she scrambled out of the tent trying to make enough noise in the hope they would be quiet and not wake Miles. Aggie had had a difficult night overthinking the Doug situation. Had she made a terrible mistake? This question had been going over and over in her mind for most of the night. Then, the last straw was the noise of a couple highlighting the fact that it would be quite a while before she would find herself in a loving relationship.

After a noisy flip flopped walk to the toilet, Aggie arrived back at the pitch to find all was quiet. She surveyed the tent and found, to her relief, that it had survived the storm. Would she survive the holiday and the immediate future of singledom she pondered as she settled herself down on a camp chair to prepare and eat her breakfast.

This time she had been organised and bought croissants from a boulangerie the day before. Not quite as good as really fresh ones but she could savour them nonetheless. She had two and enjoyed them with a large mug of fresh black coffee. To Aggie this was the perfect way to start the day. Combining it with sitting outside on a warm sunny morning placed her in heaven.

The sound of traffic on the nearby road vied for Aggie's attention but she resolutely focussed on the tranquillity of the campsite

77

which was punctuated by the sound of birdsong. From time to time a chaffinch would edge forward in an attempt to pinch a croissant crumb before flying off. Then it would return and start the process all over again. Aggie watched the bird and smiled at it. She hadn't quite reached the point of talking to wild birds like her aunt Betty.

In the shower, Aggie undressed and reflected on what Doug had said. Looking at her naked body for the first time in months, she saw the fat on her belly and cellulite on her thighs. Why hadn't she noticed this before? Doug was right. What man would ask her out looking like this? She didn't want to lower her standards and get any old man because that was all that was on offer.

She had clearly taken her eye off the ball where her fitness was concerned. Her mind had been taken over by juggling Doug's increasingly infrequent requests to see her, her sons and her inability to come up with a new and exciting body of work.

Tears started to roll down her face as she went into full 'pity party' mode. She had visions of herself still single at 70. Oh God, she was going to end up like her aunt Betty. Betty had been single since the age of 60 after having been unceremoniously dumped by her ex-husband in favour of some greedy slapper old enough to be his daughter. Since then, she had been drinking to excess, causing trouble, eating road kill as well as brewing some very strange alcoholic drinks from foraged berries.

She finished washing herself and wrapped her 'not quite big enough' microfibre towel around her body, leant against the shower cubicle wall and phoned Celia.

"Oh God, I have just looked at my naked body in the shower and Doug was right. No decent man would be interested in me."

Journey by Liz Garnett

"Are you having a 'pity party'?"

"Yes! A major one!"

"Doug is a complete plonker. He only said that because no one is going to look at him," came the sympathetic voice of Celia.

"He will get dates because he has pots of money and can afford to take them out to nice restaurants."

"Precisely! He has to buy company! They won't last long unless they are gold diggers. And, they would be bored rigid," came the wise words of Celia.

"Mmmm, I suppose so."

"Did you look at your body in a mirror?"

"No. Why?"

"Oh, you stupid mare! Foreshortening! Looking down at your body, it will always look worse. You will look slimmer if you stand up straight and look in a mirror! Also you look perfectly fine fully clothed, so what are you worried about?" said the ever supportive Celia.

"I am worried the next boyfriend I find will run a mile when I take my clothes off," came Aggie's reply as she clung to her 'pity party'.

"Forget that bit for the time being and start working on getting fit. By the time you are whipping your clothes off in a frenzy of passion you will be fine."

"I am worried I am not going to manage that and will end up like Betty," replied Aggie still clinging on to her 'pity party' for dear life.

"Are you still in this 'pity party'?"

"Yes! I am going all out with party streamers and a disco ball," replied a determined Aggie.

"Your aunt has a great life. She has freedom and her little dalliance with Bert from the allotments gives her great pleasure. She has got the balance right between hanky panky, free vegetables and not having to tidy up after him or wash his smalls."

"Yes, I suppose you are right. Poor Bert. It sounds as though he has got the short straw."

"Yes! Sex slave and provider of vegetables! What does she give in return?"

"The odd bottle of sloe gin, but I think less and less of that now that Richard has reached 18. He seems to be acquiring bottles in return for gardening services or Xbox tutorials! Thank you for cheering me up."

"My pleasure. You don't need a man at the moment. Enjoy being single. Enjoy the freedom."

With that, Aggie put the phone down and started to plan their day. With the worry of dumping Doug off her mind she was starting to feel more inclined to do some sketching. It amazed her that the simple act of 'giving him the push' had resulted in her desire to pick up a pencil and start drawing. A trip to the local art shop was in order, she decided.

As Miles was getting up and organised, Aggie reflected on her good points. Things weren't as bad as they had seemed earlier. The sun was now shining which always helped with her mood. She might have a few wrinkles and be carrying a few extra pounds but she was a better catch than she had been in her twenties. She had more confidence and she had more about her. Her sons still enjoyed her company and found her fun. She had a good group of friends and a wide network of artists and other creative friends. Yes, she thought, she was a good catch. Doug had just been lashing out now that he too would have to get back on the dating scene.

Aggie found the art shop in Rue Amiral Ronarc'h with ease and parking couldn't have been better with spaces alongside the row of shops that the art shop inhabited. The building was relatively new and topped off by an apartment block. It wasn't the prettiest part of town but it did offer untold riches in the form of the contents of the shop.

Miles stayed in the car while Aggie went into the shop. Walking through the door she was transported into heaven. A heaven of all manner of art materials. Poor Miles would be waiting in the car for some time, thought Aggie. She breathed in the smell of art paraphernalia and surveyed the shop before heading to the paints section. The smell was intoxicating and Aggie was transported back to the heady days of university where the buzz of creativity had fired the neurons in her brain. It had been a time of maximum inspiration aided by the collaboration of fellow art students. She had been driven by deadlines and existed on too much alcohol, caffeine and too little sleep. Her progress around the shop was slow as she inspected paints, papers, pencils and more. She took in the vibrancy of the colours and textures of the papers. Finances dictated that she could to only buy essential materials: A sketchbook, pencils and coloured inks. Then she added a set of pastels. She was returning to her 'happy place'.

With her art supplies safely stashed in the boot of the car, Aggie drove into the main part of town and found the car park near the multiplex cinema. They headed towards the Cathedral in search of some galleries.

Walking down Rue du Font they came across their first Quimper gallery. Stopping to look in the window, Miles sidled up to Aggie.

"If you say 'Jeremy Corbyn' three times, he appears out of nowhere and lectures you on communism," he said with his best poker face. Aggie laughed while Miles remained straight-faced but raised his eyebrows in recognition of a successful comedy moment.

"What happens if you say phwarr, phwarr, phwarr?" asked Aggie, getting into the swing of the latest game.

"No idea."

"Boris Johnson appears and lectures you on how to get fired and still be successful," replied Aggie.

After a particularly unsuccessful trawl of the Quimper galleries, they headed away from the centre of town in search of food. Aggie was still tired as they walked into the large Carrefour close to the campsite. Tired? No. She was exhausted. Thankfully, Miles had kindly offered to cook supper. She remembered past holidays where they had participated in 'Come Dine With Me' supper challenges. Both boys had been at primary school at the time. They had enjoyed the TV show in which the 'presenter' made disparaging remarks about the contestants. Aggie hated the rudeness of the 'presenter' but was thankful to the programme for giving the boys an enthusiasm for cooking on holiday. Back then the main courses had been simple. Perhaps just merguez sausages with vegetables. However, it was the puddings that showed the boys' creative skills to the full. Mostly these had been recipe free concoctions of biscuits and melted chocolate topped with mini marshmallows and sprinkles. In fact, anything that was sweet was considered a potential ingredient. Aggie wondered what Miles had in store for her that night.

Miles had absolutely no idea what he was going to cook for his mother. Pudding was out as it would make too much washing-up and he suspected Aggie would appreciate it if he did both the cooking and the washing-up. A one pot 'special' might be the best option for him along with a large baguette to cancel out any potential hunger pangs later on.

Walking through the lingerie area of the supermarket Aggie was reminded of the time she had been shopping for underwear in Marks and Spencer in Ashford. Miles had been with her and she had had the unfortunate situation of bumping into fellow artist, Malcolm, while looking at a particularly unsexy pair of body slimming knickers. She had managed not to blush as she had quickly put down the offensive item and turned to chat to Malcolm. Miles had been minding his own business up until that point but saw Malcolm's arrival on the scene as an opportunity to get a man's perspective on the wide selection of lacy bras and knickers.

"What do you think of these, Malcolm?" asked the nine-year-old Miles, holding up a purple and pink ensemble with padded uplift bra in size 36H.

"Errr umm," came the embarrassed reply from Malcolm.

"Feel the fabric on these?" continued Miles as he held up and felt a particularly silky pair of scanty panties. Malcolm was visibly embarrassed. Malcolm had no children.

"Now you just have to feel these ones," persisted Miles.

"Miles, I don't think Malcolm is interested in the underwear," said Aggie trying to ease Malcolm's embarrassment. She had struggled not to laugh. She could never understand why the lingerie department was placed in the middle of a thoroughfare and vowed to buy all her underwear online in future.

As the day progressed, Aggie was starting to feel more human. After they had jointly washed up the dishes from lunch, Aggie headed over to the empty children's play area and sat on one of the rocking seats for children aged 2-6. Miles smiled, At last, his mother was returning to her playful self. They spent a happy hour trying out all the play equipment and laughing when one or other got stuck.

They followed this by a leisurely walk along the banks of the river that bordered the campsite. The fresh air and gentle exercise was starting to lift Aggie's mood. The view of the river, although not particularly interesting was enough to give her the necessary 'get up and go' to pick up her sketchbook after the walk. Miles joined her with the drawing and they spent a couple of hours in a companionable silence punctuated by comments on their work.

Later, sitting around the camp stove, Aggie watched Miles as he prepared supper. They were having a simple bean soup with fresh vegetables into which they would dunk chunks of fresh baguette. Miles finely sliced an onion and chucked it into the pan having added a glug of olive oil. He briefly stirred the contents of the pan and then lit the stove. Aggie turned down the heat and continued to stir the pot while Miles peeled and sliced a couple of carrots, chopped some tomatoes and garlic and added these to the pan. After pouring some water into the pot, Aggie then took the can of beans to the sinks to rinse before returning and putting them into the pan.

"Smells good," said Aggie.

"Thanks. I added a stock cube and some of those dried chillis while you were away," replied Miles.

"How many?"

"Just six."

"Shit. It is going to be hot then!"

After their post supper evening walk when they were settled back in their camp chairs outside their tent, Miles looked across at Aggie. They were sitting at right angles to each other enjoying the sights and sounds of the campsite in a companionable silence. Suspicious of a distinct whiff coming from under his armpits, Miles raised one arm and sniffed, looked at Aggie and said: "musky!" in a low husky voice.

"You revolting child!" laughed Aggie. "Go and have a shower and do a good job of cleaning your pits. I am not sharing a tent with you smelling like that!" Miles laughed. If Richard had been there he would have taken off his t-shirt, rubbed it liberally in his smelly arm pits and then tried to rub it in Richard's face. He didn't think he could do the same thing to his mother. There was nothing for it but to have a shower.

Leaving Miles to settle and read his book, Aggie picked up hers. She was enjoying reading Monsieur Pamplemouse Afloat by Michael Bond and taking her mind off men. She had just read one paragraph when the phone pinged to indicate a text had come in. She harrumphed fearing it would be a text from Doug. Thankfully, it was her friend in France, Sally.

> Sally – How goes it? How is Brittany and how is your pilgrimage?

> Aggie – Weather is not great. Pilgrimage is 'interesting'. I have dumped Doug.

> Sally – Fantastic! So pleased you have dumped him. He was such a wet blanket when I met him with you at Christmas. You can do much better than him.

> Aggie – Thanks. Miles was equally thrilled and called him a 'dickhead'! However good it was to dump him, I am still feeling emotionally sore.

> Sally – It will pass. I am going to have a celebratory glass of champagne for my dinner. There are plenty more fish in the sea. Just you wait. Before that you have to find your authentic self. Tell me about the pilgrimage.

> Aggie – Well, having dumped Doug I have started to find the energy and enthusiasm for my art. Today, I bought some art materials.

> Sally – Brill. Where are you at the moment?

Aggie – Quimper – I have drawn some preliminary sketches and inspiration is coming back.

Sally – What are you drawing?

Aggie – Landscapes and some architectural ones. All very loose but I am also playing around with colour. I saw a fabulous exhibition of paintings by Jean Duquoc in Vannes. Amazing.

Sally – I saw a Duquoc exhibition some years ago. Love his work too. Can you send me some images of your work? I would love to see them.

Aggie – Will do. Give me a couple of days. How goes it at your end?

Sally – Slow. Just stuck in the studio all day at the moment. I need to escape. Must dash. Dogs are demanding an evening stroll.

Aggie felt more cheerful after Sally's texts and picked up her sketchbook to look at her day's work. Her new sketches had been quick black ink drawings with touches of colour. She had used photos from her point and shoot camera as a reference point for some architectural and landscape sketches. The contrast between these and her still life oil paintings was marked. They could have been created by a completely different artist. Reflecting on their difference, Aggie felt pleased with what she had produced so far. She had wanted new inspiration and a new body of work and this looked distinctly like the beginnings of a new style. She was pleased.

Week 1 – day 7 – Quimper

At last Aggie had had a good night's sleep. She had only needed to go to the toilet twice in the night which was a record for her. Over the last week she had found herself going three or even four times in the night which was why in the past she had restricted sleeping under canvas to a maximum block of three nights on holiday. After four nights of broken sleep she was incapable of stringing a sentence together. What planet had she been on when she decided to spend three weeks under canvas, she wondered? She had no choice but to make it work. She had very little savings left and she was not going home early - no matter how tired she was.

6.30 am was the best part of the day. All the other campers were fast asleep. Miles was also asleep. Aggie sat by her camp stove and poured water into the pan and lit the gas burner.

The sound of the gas igniting and the gentle hiss of the gas flames lit Aggie's senses. She scooped fresh coffee into her cafetière and inhaled the strong aroma of Taylors Hot Java coffee grounds. Bliss.

Aggie sat enjoying the early morning tranquillity of the campsite. The smell of damp vegetation being warmed by the first rays of the morning sun was invigorating. The sky was blue and promising a warm day ahead of them. The sound of birdsong was starting to be drowned out by the nearby main road. Aggie focussed on filtering out the traffic noise in favour of focusing on the wildlife and greenery.

Miles emerged from his slumber at 8 am and, in a bleary fug, plonked himself down on his camping chair and tucked into his croissant. Aggie took down the tent and packed up the car as speedily as she could manage while Miles ate his 'p'tit dej'. She wanted to get on the road as quickly as possible so they could enjoy the landscape and spend some time sketching enroute.

As they drove north and the road started to climb the hills that divided the north from the south of Brittany, Aggie reflected on how she was feeling. Now that she had done the deed and dumped Doug she felt a bit lost. She knew in her heart of hearts that she was better off without him but society really did prefer people to be paired off. Relief poured over her with the realisation that, as they hadn't been living together there wouldn't be any of the splitting of assets. She had also been careful not to leave any of her possessions at his house. A clean break. No future messiness.

The outside air temperature was starting to rise above 24°C. With the windows down, Aggie was managing well without the air conditioning. In fact, she was glad of the heat and a chance to really warm up. Aggie hoped that no other part of the car would pack up before the end of their holiday.

Aggie enjoyed car journeys with her son as, often as not, they threw up some interesting topics of conversation. However, on this occasion Miles was still pursuing the dating line of enquiry.

"Tony Blair or Jeremy Corbyn?" asked Miles.

"For Prime Minister?" questioned Aggie.

"No! Which one would you rather date?"

"Really Miles! I am not desperate!"

"How about Boris Johnson?"

Journey by Liz Garnett

"Seriously?"

"Okay. What about Nigel Farage?"

"Okay then. Who would you date? Theresa May?" asked Aggie turning the tables on Miles.

"Muuum! That is just stupid!"

"Precisely! Would you really want Boris, Jeremy or Nige as your step Dad?" There really was no answer to this but it did leave Miles pondering the advantages of a rich step Dad and one that would be up for a good political debate.

Miles had once quizzed his grandfather on potential future step sons and had been rewarded with a positive response for Nigel Farage. His grandfather thought that Nige would be good for lively political discussions at the local pub. Betty had been horrified at her brother's idea of a good time.

Aggie continued to drive through the mountainous region of Les Monts d'Aree until they reached the base of Mont Saint Michel. They parked in the parking area just off the main road and unloaded their picnic, art materials and camp chairs. They trudged up to the top of the 'mont' where the little chapel surveyed the landscape.

"I'm starving," said Miles.

"Let's eat first," said Aggie getting out the thermos and putting it on the ground before getting out the food. They sat with their backs to the chapel looking out over the Finistère countryside.

It was hot and humid, so Aggie took off her crumpled cardigan and rested it on the back of her chair.

Miles looked at his mother's arms and poked her 'bat wings'.

"You could fly higher than the chickens with those," he said.

"Get lost!"

"Seriously! Add a few feathers and you might even be able to fly as high as that eagle up there!" he continued, pointing at a buzzard-like bird soaring above them.

"That's not an eagle. It looks like a Western Marsh Harrier or a Hen Harrier. You are going the right way for me to leave you here!"

"Only joking!"

"It's not funny."

"You are too fat to be able to get any lift even with good thermals!"

To this, Aggie tapped Miles on his back with his half of the baguette. Miles was clearly missing Richard and opportunities to 'pull his leg'. He had an ability to make her laugh even when he was being very rude.

"Soz."

Aggie and Miles then spent their meal in companionable silence looking out at the view of green hills stretching out in front of them. It was a peaceful scene with just the sound of bird song or Miles chomping on his baguette to break the silence.

Once their meal was over, they started sketching and chatted sociably for a couple of hours.

"Doug was such a dick," Miles said, out of the blue.

"Thanks, darling, I would rather you didn't use that word."

"Doug?"

"No, Dick."

"You said it! I'm off the hook!" Miles enjoyed this kind of conversation.

"No you are not."

"Well, he was awful, then."

"Why do you say that?"

"He barely spoke to us and looked at us as if we were odd."

"Perhaps you are?"

"Piss off!"

"Don't swear."

"He was the odd one."

"Well, I agree that he didn't fit into our mad cap family."

"Why are you being so polite about him?" Miles asked, mystified.

"I can't see the point in slagging him off. The relationship is over and I want to move on."

"Good. For a minute I thought you were going to beg him to go back out with you," said a relieved Miles.

"No! Definitely not!"

With that, Aggie decided to pack up and change the subject. She didn't want thoughts of Doug dampening her mood. She wanted to stay positive and cheerful now that the weather was set fair and hopefully they would have good weather for the rest of the holiday.

As they drove towards the outskirts of Saint Pol de Léon, Aggie reflected on the perfectly smooth rural French roads – so unlike the ones in Kent. How on earth could anyone drive while applying full makeup, drink a cup of coffee and not end up looking like, or being, a road traffic accident in Kent, wondered Aggie.

The sun continued to shine as they crossed under the N12 autoroute and headed along the rural roads towards Saint Pol. They were tuned into France Bleu Bretagne on the radio and Aggie had been letting the combination of French music and conversation wash over her on the journey. Then the familiar sound of Dean Martin singing 'That's Amore' came on the radio. Aggie started to sing along much to the horror of Miles. His mother was completely tuneless but was thoroughly enjoying the opportunity to sing her heart out. Getting the gist of the chorus, Miles decided to join in with his own version:

"When your Mum is an old bag,

And she looks like a hag,

Journey by Liz Garnett

That's amore"

The cheeky bugger, thought Aggie, following with:

"When your sons an old fart,

And sounds just like Bart,

That's Amore"

This is fun, thought Miles and countered with:

"When you are high with your homies,

And have had weed brownies,

That's Amore"

The both laughed at their silliness. And continued to laugh as they drove into Saint Pol in search of the campsite.

The sat nav took them on a route through the centre of Saint Pol de Léon and then down the hill towards the sea. From the route they caught tantalising glimpses of an azure blue sea at low tide. The sea was punctured by rocky islets.

Pulling into the campsite, Aggie was relieved to find it was small and quiet. Within ten minutes of arrival they were setting up the tent. Then it was a dash to the supermarket for food. Aggie was beginning to wish they had a mini fridge and didn't have to make so many frequent trips to the shops.

Super U was easy to find and Aggie was relieved it wasn't too big. Even so, she found herself walking past the household items aisle by mistake. Then she spotted a toilet plunger and was immediately transported back to a holiday when the boys were five and seven. They had been in a similar supermarket in Honfleur and the boys had each picked up a toilet plunger and had had such fun playing with them in the supermarket. Seeing their enjoyment, Aggie had bought the boys one each. It had made a pleasant change from adding to their Lego collection. Richard and Miles had then been the only children running around the campsite with toilet plungers. At the time, Teletubbies, had been Miles' favourite TV programme and Richard had stuck one plunger to his head 'à la Teletubbies'. Not to be outdone, Miles had suctioned one to his tummy in an attempt to impersonate a Dalek from Dr Who. The fun had continued into the evenings with Richard getting one so suctioned to his tummy when he was in bed that he couldn't get off. Aggie remembered fondly that night when all she had wanted to do was to read her book. The boys had been too excited for her to have any successful 'wind down' time.

Aggie was awoken from her memories by Miles returning with a large quantity of fresh, cooked prawns. He was clearly determined to make the most of the delicious food in the supermarket.

Walking out of the supermarket, Aggie found they were walking behind an elderly lady pushing a trolley laden with heavy shopping bags. Aggie tapped her on her shoulder and offered to help her get her bags into her car. Accepting the offer, the lady chatted to Aggie and Miles as they walked to her car. On finding out that Aggie and Miles were English, she proceeded to tell them all about her life in the resistance and then how she managed after the war as a single parent with three boys. They chatted about the difficulties of being a single mother and compared their experiences. By this time, Miles had zoned out. Yet again his mother was chatting to a complete stranger in French. He let the beats of The White Stripes drown out the conversation and just smiled and nodded when he thought it was appropriate leaving the old woman in no doubt that the English teenager was one croissant short of a 'p'tit dej'.

After supper, Aggie and Miles headed out for a walk along the beach. The coastline was rocky with quiet sandy coves. Miles decided to have a go at peeing his name in the dry sand. This was a change from his usual habit of writing rude words and phrases in wet sand. Aggie walked away doing her usual 'he's not with me' act. Poor Miles, Aggie reflected. He really was missing Richard.

Returning to the campsite they chatted to a German couple with a fox terrier and a campervan before heading to bed. Dogs always gave Aggie an excuse to stop and chat to the owners and conversations were often fruitful with the exchange of travel tips and recommendations of places to visit.

Week 2 – day 8 – Saint Pol de Léon

Miles crawled out of the sleeping compartment of the tent and plonked himself down on the chair beside Aggie.

"Are you ready for breaky?" asked Aggie having already had hers.

"Yeah," grunted Miles.

"Well, put the pan on with enough water for two cups of tea. Your croissant is just here. Please make me a cup of coffee while I go and drop the kids off at the pool."

"Uhhh?"

"I am just going for a poo."

"Oh Mum! Too much information!"

"I thought I would get you back for all the rude things you say to me."

After breakfast, Aggie and Miles walked into the cathedral in Saint Pol and immediately parted company. The tranquil atmosphere washed over Aggie as she stood in the central aisle and took in the architecture and space of the building. She focused on her breathing before making her way around the cathedral in search of the relics of Saint Paul Aurélien. Finding his chapel, she stood and took in the individual aspects of the chapel and the relics of the saint. Aggie then found a pew and sat down to pray. She prayed again for her friends and family and then her mind wandered off. She was incredibly lucky for having such supportive friends who had been there for her when times were tough. She had been there for Celia too and between them they had made a great support team. Magda had been equally amazing and always had cups of tea and tissues on hand and had never passed judgement over Aggie's parenting or lifestyle choices. Being single, Aggie had learnt who to trust and who her true friends were. She had developed a strong network of support. Her aunt, Betty, had also been brilliant in her own eccentric way. Although Aggie appreciated the never ending supply of sloe gin and elderberry wine, she hadn't really appreciated the rabbit stew or badger broth. Aggie admired Betty's road kill cooking but just didn't want to eat it herself.

Then she reflected on her two lovely sons. Both were turning into fine young men. They were funny and good company and she couldn't have wished for better.

With Richard heading to university in September, the family unit and dynamic was changing. Time had passed so quickly while Richard was in sixth form and now Miles was about to embark on his A'level studies. Before she knew it, both boys would have 'flown the nest' and she would be on her own. Both Doug and Aggie had imagined that this would be the time when they would do even more together. Doug had been planning to do consultancy work for part of the year. He had even suggested she move in with him so his costs would be lower. He had expected her to rent out her house and live on the income. Now the children-having-flown-the-nest time would be empty. She saw a big blank void filling her time between children at home and death. A tear rolled down her cheek at the thought. Why was she having a 'pity party', she thought to herself. She should see this as a blank canvas to fill with things that she enjoyed. That was what she needed to do. She told herself that she needed purpose and through that purpose would come joy. With singledom came freedom without compromise.

Miles, standing some way from Aggie caught her wiping tears from her cheek and eyes. Oh God, he thought, I will have to give her a hug in public to cheer her up. How embarrassing.

Aggie saw Miles and went over to join him. They then spent an hour sketching inside the cathedral before heading out into the bright sunlight.

Coming out of the cathedral, Aggie and Miles were confronted by an elderly woman leading a goat.

"Bonbons?" she said holding up a packet of sweets followed by "cinq euros."

"English," came Aggie's reply. Bloody hell! They were expensive, thought Aggie. There was no way she was going to admit she could speak French. There was a mad look in the woman's eye and Aggie wanted to escape before the old woman decided to put a curse on them.

Aggie and Miles then wandered around the market. Aggie's mind started to wander onto her lack of finances. Market food was not cheap, but the experience of a market was all part of being in France. It's slower pace lent itself to the process of being on a pilgrimage. Then, by chance, she came across an artist selling small works of art. She stopped and looked at his work and saw a leaflet offering outdoor art classes for 40 euros. This seemed a bit steep to Aggie who was used to the price of art classes in Kent being far more reasonable. However, this started to get Aggie's brain whirring. Could this be a possible source of income for her in Kent? Targeting it correctly, it could be one income stream and she could do weekly art classes at the village hall too. Aggie started to brighten up at the thought of not being quite so poor and, more importantly, being financially secure.

Just as Aggie started to head towards the bread stall, Miles sidled up to her.

"Look over there," he said pointing at an elderly man with a flat cap. "It's Victor Meldrew." They both laughed as they watched the grumpy man walk ahead of them with a walking stick which he was using to bash shoppers legs if they got in his way.

Before leaving the market, they bought fresh pâté, cheeses, fruit and vegetables as well as five bottles of farm cider. Miles refused to carry any more. Aggie was disappointed but grateful that he was doing any carrying at all.

Miles and Aggie spent the afternoon on the beach sketching and relaxing. The sun shone down on them and Aggie was beginning to feel blessed. Looking out into the little bay, Aggie could see a man struggling to get the engine of his little boat to start. The boat was floating around aimlessly on the sea. Watching the scene reminded Aggie of her own situation. She was currently rudderless thanks to not having a boyfriend. Although, sitting there musing on her situation, she asked herself why she needed a man in her life to give her direction.

As a child she had been fed the fantasy that girls needed to get married and then they would live happily ever after. That hadn't been the case for her and focusing on having a man in her life had affected her career. Looking out to sea gave her a clearer insight now. Spending time travelling around Brittany was also helping to give her understanding about herself. As she sat there she began to realise that she needed to have art as her anchor and any man that came into her life would be an added extra that would have to work with that and not expect her to be anchored to him. Just then her phoned beeped with an incoming text.

Magda – How's the holiday?

Aggie – Improving. Weather much better. Sketching going well. How's life in Kent?

Magda – All good here. Heard an interesting fact on the radio today. Did you know 7 out of 10 members of the Conservative party are men. Mostly over 50 too.

Aggie – And why are you telling me this?

Magda – Join it! It could be a happy hunting ground for a new man in your life.

Aggie – Seriously? They will be all crusty old farts! The single ones are probably members as they lead sad and boring lives.

Magda – LOL. I shall sign you up for Christmas.

Aggie – Don't you dare! Or I will find you an equally repellent Christmas present!

That evening, as Aggie was washing-up the supper dishes, a German woman in her 30s joined her at the sinks. Seeing that Aggie's washing-up liquid was English, the woman struck up a conversation with Aggie in English. Before long they had discovered that they were both single mothers. They exchanged names and Greta told Aggie that her son was three years old and they were doing a six week grand tour of France before she started a new job in Berlin in September. Aggie expressed amazement that Greta was travelling with a three-year-old over such a long period of time. She then felt proud of the woman for the bravery she felt Greta had in travelling in such a way. It was a pride born out of the single mother's sisterhood. When the boys had been young Aggie had stuck to staying in budget chain hotels or mobile homes run by UK camping companies. She would never have dreamt of camping under canvas with them.

Aggie felt inspired. So many people in Kent had told her that she had been brave travelling to France with the boys when they were younger. Greta took this to a whole new level. This made Aggie realise that she needed to learn from this woman's strength and understand that she was capable of doing more.

Aggie and Greta finished their washing-up and conversation by exchanging emails in case they didn't have the opportunity to chat again before moving on.

Arriving back at the tent, Aggie found Miles in bed watching YouTube videos. She then headed off to the sanitary block to change. She was looking forward to a good night's sleep.

Week 2 – day 9 – Saint Pol de Léon

Aggie slowly woke to the sound of movement on the mattress next to hers. Light was streaming through the thin tent material. She could hear amorous pigeons in the process of their mating rituals, reminding Aggie of her newly celibate status. She took a deep breath and kept her eyes closed trying to remain in a semi-conscious state for as long as possible. However, the sound of a zip being undone and the quilted material of a sleeping bag being flapped about caused Aggie to open her eyes to see what was going on.

"What are you doing?" began Aggie. "Oh my God! Miles! That fart smells worse than a French sewer!" Chocking on the smell, Aggie held her breath, unzipped her sleeping bag and then unzipped the sleeping compartment and fell into the small chamber beyond. She took a deep breath of damp but un-smelly air and continued her protest. "Couldn't you have held it in and waited until you got outside the tent?"

"It wasn't me – it was the dog," came the reply. Aggie wondered if they had a dog if it would blame it's farts on Miles.

Aggie and Miles spent a peaceful day walking along the coast and sketching the scenery. The weather had improved dramatically since their first arrival in Brittany. Supper had been another of Miles' 'one pot specials' followed by a game of cards.

Feeling calmer than she had in months, Aggie left Miles in bed surfing the internet on his mobile and got into her car so she could catch up with Celia and find out about her love life. Now that she was single again she needed to have some positive stories to give her hope. Knowing what she did about the single scene for her age group she doubted the news would be good but at least there was a chance of a giggle.

"So, tell me how the date went?" asked Aggie.

"Awful," came the reply.

"No!"

"I sat there opposite him and thought 'is this all I am good for?' He was at least 10 years older than he claimed and his photo must have been taken 20 years ago!"

"No!" giggled Aggie.

"Then he had this pot belly on him that looked like a large pudding bowl. His tummy was even poking out between the buttons of his shirt and to cap it all off he dyes his hair black!" replied Celia, barely able to contain herself.

"Ugghh! How awful! You deserve better than that. There must be someone better out there. Anything on Tinder?"

"Well, I have been madly swiping left," replied Celia.

"Is that good or bad? I haven't even tried Tinder yet."

"Left is reject, right is phwaw or has potential."

"How do you decide from just a photo?" enquired Aggie.

"Well, there are usually more than one photo and I do as follows: tattoos – swipe left. Half-naked and no hairy chest – swipe left.

Half-naked and a veritable forest – swipe right. Photos that include other women – swipe left."

"Seriously? They include pictures of other women?"

"Yes, bizarre isn't it? I would be hopping mad if an ex of mine included a picture of me with him on one of these sites. Children are also included and if my ex did that I would be fuming!"

"I agree!"

"There are even ones of men holding up large fish that they have caught as if they are offering up gifts to the gods."

"Do you swipe left or right for those ones?"

"I refuse to dignify that question with an answer! There was even one of a guy lying on a beach lounger showing off his fine beer belly which rolled over the top of his speedos. Why? Why? Why?"

" I certainly can't answer that question! You have not given me any hope with the current dating situation. I shall have to become a nun!"

"Perhaps we need to try speed dating or singles parties again," suggested Celia, hopeful that Aggie would join her in another adventure.

"Great idea! Do you remember that singles party we went to in Canterbury?"

"The one where we were mistaken for the event organisers?"

"Yes. All because we were doing such a good job of introducing other singles," replied Aggie. "Do you remember that guy who was in his 40s who told us the story of one of his internet dating disasters?"

"Which one was that?" came Celia's reply as she tried to work out who Aggie was talking about. They had met so many people that night.

"The guy who had arranged a date with a woman he thought was in her 40s but she turned out to be 70."

"Oh yes! We laughed like drains! I don't think we were meant to laugh."

"No. I think we were meant to be sympathetic. You have to laugh at these situations otherwise you end up becoming depressed."

"I agree," replied Aggie.

"I wonder what they make of us," pondered Celia.

"I dread to think what they think of me!" laughed Aggie. "Do you remember that one internet first date I went on where I had to pretend I was a clinical psychologist and that it was important for me to analyse his true feelings before we could move forward?"

"Oh yes! What was the reason for that? I forget."

"He kept telling me I was beautiful and how he thought we would make beautiful babies together. Having only just met him it just seemed a bit odd. Particularly as I wasn't looking my best as I had had very little sleep the night before. The bags under my eyes could have carried a week's worth of groceries. I smelt a rat. No man is that keen on a first date."

"What was his reaction?"

"He suddenly found he had to go."

"How funny! I must remember that when I need to extricate myself," replied Celia, thinking it was good to have an easy way of letting a man down. "I must say there are a good number of men who tell me about the awful first dates that they have been on. From what they have said, some of these women are truly awful."

"I know. It always makes me want to laugh when they recount tales of dates with women that they describe as 'nutcases'. Where do these women come from? Certainly, all my single female friends are lovely and any man going on a date with one of them would be very lucky."

"I do hope you are including me in the group of 'lovely friends'."

"Of course!"

Laughing they both felt more cheerful despite their disastrous love lives.

Ending the call, Aggie clambered into bed and wished Miles goodnight. His reply was a grunt as he was engrossed in a Youtube video.

What had first drawn her to Doug on that dating website, she wondered? Looking back on it she couldn't remember. Perhaps he had been one of the few to strike up a conversation with her. There hadn't been any other dates around at the time they went on their first date. She remembered sitting opposite him in a pub that day. She had felt sorry for him. That was certainly not a good start. She needed to get a grip and not date any man who gave her the lost puppy dog eyes. She needed a man who was independent and didn't need her to provide him with entertainment.

Needing entertainment had been a big no no. She had sat opposite a good number of men on first dates that had been looking for a woman to provide them with a readymade social life. She wasn't prepared to act as their entertainer or carer. She wanted to be in a relationship where she was an equal.

Week 2 – day 10 – Saint Pol de Léon

Aggie was woken by the sound of the next door tent being taken down. It was 6.30 am but she didn't feel like staying in bed so clambered out of the sleeping compartment and pulled on a pair of jeans.

Once out of the tent she said hello to her neighbours. They told her about the forecast for heavy rain, so Aggie decided to have a shower before breakfast and see if she could get Miles to stir his stumps earlier than usual.

Just as Aggie was leaving the shower block the heavens opened. She rushed back to their tent and started to prepare breakfast with the aid of an umbrella to keep the rain off the camp stove while she boiled some water.

The rain continued and was joined by thunder and lightning. After breakfast under canvas, Miles came into his own by being more helpful and efficient than usual in getting packed. Just as they had packed up the bedding and were loading it into the car, Greta wandered past and came over to offer help. Between the three of them they made light work of pulling out tent pegs and easing tent poles out of their sleeves.

Water streamed through the pitch and made the folding of the tent a soggy nightmare. They would be taking a large quantity of rainwater with them on their journey. For the umpteenth time Aggie wondered what on earth she was doing. By the end of the packing ordeal they were all drenched despite their rain macs. Aggie thanked Greta profusely for her help and they wished each other a safe onward journey and happy end of holidays as they bid each other farewell.

When they were finally sitting in the car with the windows misting up, Aggie took a deep breath and set the sat nav for Tréguier. It was set to rain for the whole morning and she decided to avoid the picturesque towns en route and just get to the next campsite.

The drive took in some interesting countryside and Aggie was frustrated that the rain was hiding the beauty of the landscape and villages. They pulled off the road at Plestin les Grèves to eat a couple of Kouign Amens. The parking area placed the car facing the beach and beyond to the sea. It wasn't a brilliantly healthy packed lunch but they enjoyed the sugary, butteryness of the pastries that couldn't be bought in the UK. Aggie's expanding waistline ouzed over the top of her frayed and paint splattered denium shorts. She thanked the clever use of a size 14 polo shirt that had the ability to hide her spare tyre. As they sat in the car they watched the rain pound the windscreen.

"Il pleut comme vache qui pisse," said Aggie breaking the silence.

"What?" came Miles' reply. His mind had been contemplating the future, his future. In particular the joys of sixth form and whether he could start a little business selling chocolate and cans of cola to younger students.

"I thought I would broaden your French by introducing you to a phrase about the weather," replied Aggie. "It means it is raining like a cow pissing."

"Oh yuck! Mother you are so disgusting!" Where did his mother find these revolting expressions? That wasn't one he could employ at school. No. What he really needed were expressions that sounded innocuous but could be passed on to students lower down the school for their French classes which would get them into trouble. There were a couple of cocky year 9s that needed to be taken down a peg or two.

The tide was out so they couldn't even enjoy the view of the sea. They sat in a companionable silence. The greyness of the day had flattened their mood.

Having finished their lunch, they set off for Treguier and their campsite. They only had one stop to make and that was for petrol and supper.

Aggie pulled into a supermarket petrol station on the outskirts of Lannion and swore under her breath for having no choice but to accept the E10 petrol. She had been made anxious about filling up with this petrol since the first days of it's introduction in France. Some cars had ceased to work on it and she had never been sure whether her car could or couldn't run on it. Up until this point she had managed without it but the petrol gauge was almost on empty so she would have to risk it and hope that her breakdown service would come to the rescue if the car stopped working. She was also unhappy at having no choice but to pay at the pump. She much preferred paying at a kiosk and having another opportunity of using her French to chat with whoever was behind the screen.

Then it was a quick nip into the supermarket for supper. She was beginning to get seriously bored of trawling around supermarkets on a daily basis. However, she was acutely aware of their dwindling funds and she knew that the last few days would be funded by her credit card and she would have to dump a whole load of older paintings on Ebay to raise funds to pay for any overspend. She knew that there were some well-executed college drawings and possibly, paintings, in the attic.

Driving into the campsite along a short causeway, Aggie couldn't quite believe their luck. The views across the sea to a small island were to die for. She loved the sea and couldn't wait to get out and explore the coastline. By the time Aggie and Miles emerged from the car their clothes were still damp and Aggie's shorts were chaffing her thighs. The rain had ceased and Aggie was keen to get the tent erected so it could start to dry out.

Aggie was pleased that the new campsite met with her expectations. It was small, friendly and had large tidy pitches. The summer rains had kept the campsite green and lush. Miles was not so impressed as the campsite was devoid of a swimming pool and therefore devoid of teenagers.

Once parked on their pitch, they started their well-practiced routine of erecting the tent. Unlike Aggie and Miles, the tent had had no chance to dry out so they got wet all over again as they threaded the tent poles through the soaking wet tent fabric. As Aggie rolled up the entrance to the tent to let the air circulate, the sun broke through the clouds.

"Perfect timing," said Aggie smiling up at the sun.

"Beach?" enquired Miles.

"Absolutely!" replied Aggie. "Let's take the chairs, stove and food in the car and have supper on the beach."

"Cool."

Before heading off down to the beach, Aggie and Miles stood and looked out at the view. The tide was in and the sea sparkled in the sunlight. Aggie took in a deep breath and savoured the smell of the salty air. She was in heaven.

"Shit! Look over there!" urged Miles, grabbing Aggie's arm and pointing to a man in the distance. "He's naked!"

"Where? I can't see where you are pointing."

"Over there! Are you visually challenged?"

"No, but your eyesight is much better than mine," said Aggie straining her eyes until she could see the vague shape of a naked man. "Oh my goodness. There were no signs up saying it was a nudist beach when we drove past."

"Will you bet me a thousand pounds to run along the beach naked?" came Miles' reply as he saw an opportunity to increase his bank balance.

"Would you pay me a thousand pounds to run along that beach naked?" Came Aggie's response. She was smiling but Miles couldn't see her face.

"Oh yuck! That is so gross! I don't ever want to see your naked body. I bet it is all wrinkly and saggy. Ugghh!" replied Miles who felt sick at the thought.

"Precisely," replied a laughing Aggie. "I don't want to see your naked body either."

Miles joined Aggie in laughing and, picking up their picnic and art gear, headed onto the beach and in the opposite direction of the naked man. There were no other naked bodies around so they didn't walk far before they found a spot to set up their chairs and art equipment.

They then spent an hour sketching and experimenting with different art materials. The view was calming and conveniently had an island in it to give them a point of interest. Miles was ignoring the scenery in favour of drawing some of the girls he had photographed in Vannes. He knew he would be onto a winner if he could only master the art of drawing people. To be precise, the art of drawing pretty girls. His mind then took him back home and to Folkestone and he thought of the harbour there and ruminated on the best location to sit and sketch. He wondered where the best place would be to attract the attention of attractive girls his age.

By five o'clock they decided it was time for an early supper. Miles fired up the gas stove, placed the frying pan on it and put a dollop of butter in the pan. Aggie peeled off the lid on a packed of gallettes and placed one in the frying pan once the butter had melted and was bubbling away. She then added a slice of emmental cheese and a slice of jambon de Bayonne and cooked the gallette. Once cooked, she folded over the edges and placed it onto a plate for Miles and then made one for herself. She continued this routine until all six gallettes had been cooked and eaten. This traditional Breton meal was simple but pleasurable.

Having consumed their gallettes, they sat in peaceful silence looking out to sea and discussed how the landscape had changed since their arrival. The tide was continuing to go out and before them stretched a muddy rocky expanse waiting to be explored. Leaving their possessions, they got up and wandered down to where the sea had been and started to explore and search for interesting shells.

Just as Aggie crouched down to pick up an unusual shell, a beep from her bag announced the arrival of a text.

Magda – So, is the universe rushing into that space in your head vacated by Doug?

Aggie – I am getting there. Sketchbook bought, pencils bought, inks bought. New sketches coming along nicely.

Magda – Fantastic!

Aggie – Have seen some interesting art down here. Very different to the art in Kent. Hopefully I shall produce something new and exciting. How is the pet portrait coming along?

Magda – A bloody pain in the backside! However, it is finished and I have cold hard cash in my sticky mitts so I am happy.

Aggie – Well done! Here's to our successful futures.

Getting into bed that night, Aggie reflected that it had been a good day, despite the rain. It had been fun taking down the tent in the storm and she had enjoyed how they had both worked well together as a team.

Week 2 – day 11 – Tréguier

Aggie woke at 6 am to the sound of the sea and yet more mating pigeons. She groaned and got out of bed and headed for a shower. Once refreshed she brewed a cup of coffee and left Miles fast asleep and wandered down to the beach to sit and consume her breakfast. Once on the beach she kicked off her flip flops and enjoyed the sensation of the cold sand on her bare feet. She wiggled her toes in the sand before sitting down and taking in the view and having her breakfast.

Arriving in Tréguier, Aggie chose to park near the marina and walk up into town. Tréguier is built on a hill and the streets leading away from the river are steeped in history with medieval buildings jostling for attention.

They stopped to have a look at a second-hand bookshop at the bottom of Rue Ernest Renan. Miles stood in the street photographing the buildings while thinking about how he could best capture them in charcoal. Just as Aggie was rummaging in the rows of books outside the shop, a man in his mid-seventies approached her. He was shabbily dressed in ancient brown trousers and a mac tied up with string. There was a distinct whiff coming from his direction. Aggie surreptitiously tried to move around him so she wasn't downwind. His beard and hair were unkempt and Aggie wondered when he had last had a bath and then tried to eradicate the thought of the man's wrinkled, naked body in his bath. The mental image was too repellent for words.

The man spoke to her in French and asked if she was a tourist. She replied that she was in her best French accent. The man then started to speak English, telling her that her French was very good and asking where she lived in England.

"Kent," replied Aggie trying not to encourage the man into a long conversation while thinking 'why me?' How was it Celia managed to have attractive men approach her in the supermarket and yet Aggie seemed to attract tramps. Miles had edged further away and turned his attention to filming the scene.

"I have been to England. I spent some time in Wales and Cornwall," continued the man, eager to not miss an opportunity to practice his English.

"Oh really?" said Aggie.

"Yes, I love England and I don't get much of an opportunity to speak English nowadays."

The conversation continued for a further five minutes while Aggie politely conversed in English wishing she was speaking in French.

"My name is Hervé," offered the man. "Would you like to go for a coffee?"

"I am really sorry," replied Aggie. "I have my son with me and we really must get going. Good-bye."

With that Aggie put down the book she had been considering buying and caught up with Miles who was in his element. He had sent the video to Richard along with a text message.

Miles – Mum has a new boyfriend.

Richard – No!

Miles – Yes! She is going to bring him home with us as he has nowhere to live.

Richard – Piss off.

Miles – I said to Mum he could have your room but she said he will be sleeping with her.

Richard – PISS OFF.

Miles smiled. He had successfully wound up his brother.

"Why did you abandon me, darling?" asked Aggie.

"I thought you were having a lovely time."

"No you didn't! What were you up to?"

Just then Aggie received a text from Richard.

Richard – That man is NOT moving into our house.

Aggie then turned to Miles and showed him the text. Miles smiled.

"I might have sent him a video of you chatting up that man," came Miles' sheepish reply.

"I was not chatting up that man. It was the other way around. You rotter!" Having solved the mystery of Richard's text, Aggie replied to him.

Aggie – Your brother was pulling your leg. He left me to be chatted up by the old man.

Richard – Ta. Don't bring back stray Frenchmen.

Aggie – I can't see that happening with your brother in tow.

With that Aggie and Miles headed on up the hill and sat in the main square. They spent a pleasant morning sketching the buildings and cathedral. Aggie played around with doing quick sketches of people as they passed while Miles tried out a set of new pastels. They were both making progress with their art. Aggie was developing a new style and Miles had enough pictures to make a dent in his A'level art coursework.

Heading back down towards the car, Aggie periodically stopped to take photos. The medieval buildings were inspiring her and as she took photos she was working out how she could draw them and play around with shape and colour.

Reaching the tourist shop at the bottom of Rue Ernest Renan, Aggie and Miles stopped and looked in the window and started to discuss what they should buy to take home for friends and family.

An old lady sidled up to Aggie, nudged her, fixed her with a beady stare and said "merde" before shuffling off up the street. Miles and Aggie looked at each other and laughed. Experiences like this were what made holidays special. Aggie made a mental note to add this encounter to her diary otherwise she would forget it. In the winter months, or when she was feeling sad, she would read her holiday diaries and they would cheer her up.

Celia rang Aggie just as they reached the car. So, they found a bench to sit on while Aggie chatted to Celia and Miles listened to his music.

"How cheerful are you feeling today?" she asked.

"Better, thanks."

"Ready to hit the internet dating scene?"

"Not quite! I seem to remember that men in their 40s are still on an ego trip. In their 50s, they are fine because if it was going to wither and fall off it would have done so by then. Consequently, they want a much younger woman. In their 60s, they are terrified that they haven't got much life left and anything will do. By the time they get to their 70s, they are just grateful. Then when they get to their 80s they are worried that anyone younger than them is a gold digger. Really there is no hope."

"You are so cynical!"

"Thank you! How about your dating?" Aggie enquired.

"Well, I am giving myself a gold star!"

"Oh really? What have you done?"

"I have just signed up to Match.com in the hope that I will find someone intelligent, erudite and solvent."

"Brilliant!" came Aggie's reply. "How are you finding it?"

"Not too bad but under the heading of 'qualities – honesty' who on earth would tick the box 'borders on fiction'?"

"No! Seriously? Did someone actually tick that box?"

"Yes! And, get this! My dear, beloved ex-husband has signed up and put his age at 40!"

"No! I thought he was older than you."

"Yes, the perfidious little shit is 55 if he is a day," replied Celia.

"How do you feel about seeing him on there?"

"Okay," she replied, trying not to think of him.

Once back at the campsite, Aggie decided to leave Miles to his YouTube videos and go and do some clothes washing. She was getting distinctly slovenly with her clothing as she was finding it boring trudging to the washing machines on a frequent basis. She was now wearing t-shirts for several days in a row and if, after having sniffed the armpits of a two-day-old t-shirt, she could get away with wearing it for a third day she would. Miles had no problem wearing clothes for longer than a day. He felt it was important to get into training for when he went to university.

Walking into the 'laverie', Aggie found all the washing machines were occupied.

"Merde," said Aggie.

"Sorry?" came the reply from the woman who was waiting for her washing to finish.

"All the machines are in use," replied Aggie switching to English. "Just my luck!"

"My washing will be finished in a few minutes, if you want to wait."

"Thanks. I will do that."

Aggie then decided to use the waiting time to have an adult conversation. Something she was missing now that her friends weren't around the corner for coffee and chats. She found meeting people on holiday interesting. She wondered, not for the first time, whether a part time role as a local radio presenter interviewing guests would make a good side line to her artistic career. Certainly it was better than anything that Doug had suggested.

Having established where the woman came from, Aggie went on to enquire about the woman's holiday. Much to Aggie's delight the woman was travelling around France and had interesting tales of life on the road and places visited. The woman was about 10 years older than Aggie and went on to tell her about the winter work she did training chalet girls in the French alps.

"That's very interesting," said Aggie. "I am currently at an impasse with my art career. Hearing about your work makes me realise that there are more than just 9-5 jobs as a way to earn an extra crust."

"Oh yes. I also do a stint of exam invigilation each summer at the local secondary school and I also do telephone interviewing for a market research company from time to time. I meet lots of artists, actors and writers who take on this kind of temporary work." The woman then went on to give Aggie advice on where to find more unusual jobs before going on her way.

Loading up the washing machine, Aggie felt another weight lifted off her shoulders. Here were some more options for earning money that she could fit around her painting. With the current economic climate Aggie needed to have more than one string to her bow. She also didn't want to give up her career as an artist or reduce it to weekends only.

She then sat down in one of the uncomfortable plastic chairs by the washing machine and closed her eyes to meditate while, in the back of her mind, ideas started to form of a better picture of her future.

After Aggie had hung up the washing, she dragged Miles away from his YouTube videos and took him for a walk along the beach. The tide had started to go out and they picked their way along the shoreline. At one point, they came across some samphire growing below the high tide point. Aggie reached into her capacious, orange holiday handbag and pulled out a cotton tote bag and they started to collect a small bundle of samphire for their supper.

They continued along the coastline for another half an hour before turning back. There were no other foragers out and wouldn't be until the tide was fully out. Aggie loved the closeness the French had to nature. As they walked along the beach above the high tide mark they both thought of Betty and how she would enjoy foraging on this beach.

Miles thought of how Betty had taught him to collect and then cook shellfish. At the time, he had thought she was quite mad because his primary school friends had said it was odd to forage along the seashore. After that incident, he hadn't told them of her sloe gin, elderflower wine or cider making. Now that he was sixteen he saw her differently. She was cool. All Richard's friends rated her drinks as the best they had ever tasted and even Miles enjoyed the odd glass of Betty's Superior Apple Cider. Betty, he thought, should have been born in France.

Arriving back at their pitch, they got to work preparing supper. Along with the samphire, Miles took the defrosted frozen raw prawns that they had bought earlier to rinse at the sinks. Meanwhile, Aggie got out the frying pan and added large dollops of very soft unsalted Breton butter to the pan. She then crushed two large cloves of garlic, savouring the pungent smell and noting the juiciness of each clove. She added these to the pan along with the juice of one lemon. Miles arrived back just as Aggie was lighting the gas stove. He added the prawns and samphire to the pan and took charge of stirring while Aggie broke a fresh baguette into quarters and opened them up. She then ripped the cellophane wrapping from a small iceberg lettuce and peeled off the outer leaves. Not bothering to wash the lettuce, she tore up what was left of the lettuce and inserted a generous number of leaves into each portion of baguette. Miles then added a quarter of the buttery prawns and samphire mixture to each of the baguette sections.

Turning off the stove, Aggie and Miles sat back and surveyed their meal. Aggie then cracked open a bottle of earthy farmhouse cider and poured each of them a glass. Raising their glasses they both said "cheers" before taking a sip and savouring the fresh taste of the cider.

They then turned their attention to their food. Biting into their baguettes was pure bliss for both of them. The garlic butter had soaked into the bread and the lettuce added just the right amount of crunch. Even the non-local prawns tasted good. For Aggie, the samphire tasted particularly delicious as she hadn't had to buy it.

Once supper was over and they had cleared up Miles and Aggie sat down to a competitive game of cards. They talked about their art and how much Miles' art had improved over the course of their time away.

"Your architectural sketches are really coming along, Miles."

"Thanks. I am enjoying doing them."

"Perhaps you should look into becoming an architect?"

"I was thinking of that or an artist."

"Tempted as I am to encourage you to become an artist, it is a difficult career choice and a financial struggle. You could do it alongside being an architect, for example. Being an artist is more than just drawing and painting. Nowadays, you need to be good at online marketing and Search Engine Optimisation. How about running an online shop selling your art while you are in sixth form and then at university? What do you think of that?"

"Good point. I think I have chosen the wrong A'levels for a degree in architecture."

"Don't worry. We can look at that when we get home and I know that your school will allow you to change your A'level choices up to two weeks into your first year of sixth form. Let's make sure we have a look at all that when we get home. In the meantime, you can ruminate on the idea of architecture and see how you feel when we get back. How does that sound?"

"Perfect." With that Miles then won the game of cards putting him in a good mood. There were distinct advantages of spending time with his mother. Her ability to help him see his future more clearly was one and the other was she wasn't very good at playing 21 or Vingt et Un as she insisted on calling it.

Aggie woke at 11 pm. Her bladder was demanding a visit to the toilet. She lay still for a few minutes collecting her thoughts and hoping the desire for a pee would go away. It didn't. The campsite was blissfully peaceful as she clambered out of the tent and slipped on her damp, dew soaked flip flops and headed to the sanitary block. She could hear an owl hooting in the nearby woods. Then she heard an awful snuffling sound. It wasn't quite a snarl. Could it be a rabid squirrel, she wondered, terrified. The need to go to the toilet was now more pressing and she had to be brave. The noise was also becoming louder and was definitely between her and her destination. She moved her torch around to see if she could locate it's source. Then, she saw some long grass moving vigorously by some bushes outside the sanitary block. Carefully, she moved closer, while pointing the torch at the moving grass. The noise stopped. Aggie proceeded with caution until she saw the creatures which had been making the noise. Two amorous hedgehogs. Aggie breathed a sigh of relief and chuckled to herself before nipping into the toilet before wetting herself. The natural world was continuing to remind her of her newly single status. She was less bothered now and this was a clear sign that she was starting to change.

Week 2 – day 12 – Tréguier

Aggie was walking back from having had a shower when the croissants were delivered to the tent. She had been thrilled to learn of this service on the campsite the day before and had placed her order at reception at once.

"Merci," said Aggie to the owner who was acting as 'delivery boy'. What a service, she thought. The croissants smelt amazing and were still warm. She opened their paper bag and put her nose close to the opening and inhaled. Bliss. She then sat down in her low camp chair, lit the stove and started the process of making her morning coffee. The aroma of ground coffee mixed with the sweet smell of fresh croissants. Aggie was in heaven.

Her peace and quiet was shattered as Miles emerged from the tent and slipped on his flip flops.

"Just going to drain the anaconda," he said, lowering the tone of the atmosphere to gutter level and making a dash for the sanitary block with his towel and wash bag before Aggie could respond.

Returning from his ablutions, Miles leant over Aggie and breathed over her and said: "minty fresh!" in a low, deep, breathy voice. Laughing, he clambered into the tent to get dressed for the day. Aggie felt she couldn't get too cross with him as he was clearly missing Richard and she secretly found his antics funny. She was regressing back into her childhood when she had been equally horrible to her sister. Or, had she been worse?

Walking into the Cathédral Saint Tugdual in Tréguier, Aggie was immediately relaxed by the calm atmosphere of the building.

Taking in a deep breath, she inhaled the cool air which was scented with the smell of burning candles. She was suddenly hit by the realisation that she was now over half way through her pilgrimage. Perhaps now was the time to reflect on what, if any, changes had been made in the course of the pilgrimage. Aggie went in search of the relics of Saint Tugdual and stood at the entrance to his chapel and began to reflect. It seemed to her that fear was the biggest stumbling block. Fear was holding her back. Fear of having no love. Fear of poverty. Fear of the future. Fear of no sense of purpose. How was she going to get a grip of herself? She decided to tackle each fear in turn.

Was her fear of not being loved worth worrying about, she wondered. She certainly didn't want to end up with the wrong man and she was certain it was better to be single than in the wrong relationship. So, what was it she wanted out of a relationship? A man would be a guaranteed travelling companion when Miles left home. He would also be available for walks, meals out and, most importantly of all, dealing with spiders. However, Aggie could travel and spend time with any of her many friends. She had now mastered the art of dealing with spiders. Far better to be single and happy. She had to be strong and she knew she was. Raising boys, she had had to lead from the front. Aggie took a deep breath and decided to pray for support and guidance. She would address the fears of poverty, future and sense of purpose at her next pilgrimage stops.

While she prayed, she couldn't quite escape the fear of being single. It still gnawed at her. This was also tied up with the fear of rejection. Doug had rocked her boat when he had said that no man would be interested in her at her age. What a complete shit, she thought. She got the impression that men were going for women younger than themselves. A ten or so year gap wasn't unheard of.

Journey by Liz Garnett

The last thing Aggie wanted, at the age of 50, was a 60-year-old, crusty man in need of a carer. A series of toy boys might be the answer, she pondered. She could then have some fun and then ditch them before they became boring. Then Aggie remembered that what she really needed to focus on was her career and future and not get distracted by the opposite sex.

After having prayed and had a further exploration of the cathedral and it's artworks, they walked out of the cathedral into the bright sunshine.

With their cultural fix of the cathedral completed, Aggie and Miles found an outside table at one of the cafés in the main square. They sat next to each other facing the cathedral and took in its splendour while they waited for their drinks.

Just as their coffee and hot chocolate were placed on the table, a group of attractive businessmen walked past. Aggie managed to say "merci" to the waiter at the same time as her eyes followed the men on their way to work. Miles smiled to himself, not missing a trick. Within a minute, he was handing his mother one of his headphone earbuds. She put it in her left ear and was nearly turned deaf as the Weather Girls blasted out with 'It's raining men'. Turning to Miles, Aggie laughed and smiled guiltily.

Miles looked out at the scene in the square and pointed out a man to Aggie.

"Darling, he has a beard. I am not a fan of beards," responded Aggie.

"I am not a fan of girls with beards either," added Miles. They both laughed at the daftness of the conversation.

Waking just before midnight, Aggie sighed deeply knowing that she would have to make a trip to the toilet. This time she was prepared for the sounds of romancing hedgehogs as she walked stealthily towards the toilet block. All was silent, the air was fresh with a hint of damp pine needles. As Aggie walked quietly to the towards the toilet block she breathed in the fragrant damp air. She savoured the cool air on her face. Just as she was enjoying the sensation of the air in her lungs and the tranquillity surrounding her, she tripped up. Managing to right herself without too much damage, she turned and looked down at what had been in her way. A hedgehog. Cursing the spiny creature she continued on her way.

Week 2 – day 13 – Tréguier

Aggie crawled out of the tent at 7 am to be greeted by a blue sky. The tent and all around was dew soaked. She took a deep breath and inhaled the damp scented air and then slipped on her damp flip flops and headed for a shower.

Returning to the tent, revived and ready to embrace the day, Aggie decided that the light was perfect to photograph her sketches. Placing the sketchbook on the ground, she knelt over it and photographed each page with her phone. Before having a chance to critique her work, Aggie emailed the digital files to Sally. If she didn't do it before breakfast she would find another excuse to delay. She was anxious that her new work was not as good as her old style and valued Sally's opinion. Sally had trained at the Royal College of Art and had gone on to have successful exhibitions in London before moving to France. They had met nine years earlier while Aggie was on holiday in the Loire. Aggie had been trying to encourage her, then, young sons to sit quietly outside the chateau at Blois and draw what they saw. This was part of her mission to help them gain an appreciation of art and had followed a trip around an art gallery. Sally had been impressed with the family group as they sat drawing the chateau and had wandered over to speak to Aggie. They had found they had more in common than just art and had kept in touch ever since. On Sally's frequent visits to the UK they had met for coffee or lunch and had even collaborated on a couple of exhibitions.

The sun was shining and they waited until most of the dew on the tent had evaporated before packing up. Aggie felt sad to leave such a picturesque spot and vowed to return. Even Miles was sad to leave.

Leaving Tréguier, Aggie reflected that she was getting into her stride driving on the small country roads. She had soon grasped the road rules in western Brittany which still had Priorité à Droite at some junctions making the driving experience more interesting and distinctly dangerous.

Just outside a small village they drove past a dead wild boar. Aggie could see in her rear view mirror the Frenchman in the car behind stop and pick it up. Aggie smiled as she was reminded of her aunt Betty who stalked the rural Kent roads on her mobility scooter collecting road kill or, creating and collecting it, as Aggie believed was more the case. In the autumn Betty would also raid the local hedgerows for sloes and wild plums for her famous sloe gin or plum vodka. Aggie reflected that Betty would love France and fit right into the rural way of life. Aggie had visions of her training her dog to sniff out truffles while hanging out with the local 'chasseurs'.

The weather was sunny and there wasn't a cloud in the sky so Aggie and Miles decided to stop at the coast and spend the afternoon sketching and exploring a beach. They pulled the car off at Étables sur Mer and found easy parking. Once parked, they remained in the car keeping the doors open and eating their sandwiches in silence while bathed in their own thoughts. Then Aggie looked around the interior of the car and took in how much more disgusting the car had become since the start of the journey. There were crumbs everywhere. The passenger footwell was a sea of crisp packets and chocolate bar wrappers. Ignoring the mess, they both got out of the car and headed to the beach for a few hours of art and contemplation.

Thanks to the sat nav, Aggie found the campsite at Saint Brieuc easily. Her dislike of driving in towns and cities was diminished by the use of a sat nav which eased her anxiety over getting to her destination. The campsite was set in a valley in one of the suburbs. Once parked on their pitch, Aggie and Miles set about putting up the tent and were becoming a finely tuned team. Finally, Miles had finished unloading the bedding and, having dumped it into the sleeping compartment, sat down beside Aggie to have a cup of tea and check his Instagram account. Aggie savoured the peace and quiet while texting Magda.

Aggie – I am trying to get my head around earning more money from my art. Can I bounce some ideas off you?

Magda – Of course. What like?

Aggie – Well, I need something else apart from my new body of work. I picked up an artist's leaflet at a market. It was offering expensive art classes 'plein aire'. I was thinking of doing the same but need something similar for the winter months.

Magda – Great idea. Why not do still life art classes? You can do those all year around too. Why not do them at my village hall – perhaps in the morning before my afternoon life classes.

Aggie – Great idea. Some of our clients might be interested in both classes.

Magda – We could do lunches for them.

Aggie – Brilliant. Fancy doing an evening class as well? Perhaps at another village hall?

Magda – Yes. How about joining forces and doing an after school art class at one of the local primary schools?

Aggie – Don't push it with the children! I think I will stick with adults for the time being.

Magda – LOL.

Aggie – Thanks so much. I am starting to feel much better about my future.

Magda – My pleasure. You are helping me too. This might be what I need to keep away from pet portraits. Enjoy the rest of your holidays.

Aggie – Will do.

Aggie and Miles spent a quiet evening playing cards and discussing the photos they had taken and their art. It was at times like this that had them reflecting on past holidays.

"Do you remember our holiday with Betty?"

"Yeah. That was fun," replied Miles. "I enjoyed the pêche à pied."

"Yes, it was fun but I always worry that foraging along the seashore with Betty will result in one of us being poisoned."

"Nah. She hasn't poisoned anyone yet. Do you remember that café?"

"With the rude waitress who swore at us?"

Journey by Liz Garnett

"Madam Putain as Betty called her."

"Oh yes! You kept demanding to go there every day so you could learn some more swear words." At this, Miles smiled guiltily. He wondered how his mother always managed to read his mind like a book. His knowledge of French 'gros mots' was second to none.

They continued to reminisce while Aggie, sporadically, lit incense sticks to ward off mosquitos. There weren't any but that didn't deter Aggie. The jasmine scented smoke wafted over them as Aggie went on to regale Miles with stories of student life. By the time they went to bed, the smell of sweat had been masked by jasmine smoke.

Week 2 – day 14 – Saint Brieuc

Aggie and Miles woke late to the sound of rain pounding on the roof of their tent. Aggie sighed. She had hoped to do more drawing. She picked up her smartphone and checked the weather forecast. It was due to change at around 11 am – if she was lucky and the forecast was correct. That was the problem with camping in Brittany. The weather was so varied and Aggie had to go with the flow and let the weather dictate how they spent their day.

There was nothing for it but to get dressed there and then, hit the toilet block and then find a dry café for breakfast. The campsite had a small bar that served coffee and croissants in the morning so that would have to do.

Once revived by their 'p'tit dej', Miles and Aggie decided that there was no better wet weather activity than going to the pool. It would be empty and they could both have fun on the water slide.

Aggie didn't dare get into the pool before going down the slide as she knew the water would be freezing. Dipping her toe into the icy water would have her running back to the shower block for a piping hot shower. Aggie gingerly went up the steps to the slide followed by Miles who was going to make sure she didn't change her mind. Aggie sat at the top of the slide with the cold pool water flowing past her and down the slide. She was just plucking up the courage to launch herself down the slide when Miles pushed her. She screamed as she sailed down the slide and into the freezing depths of the pool. Not only had that woken her up but she was in no doubt that it would have drawn the rest of the campers from their slumber. As Aggie's head emerged from the pool, she realised she should have known better. She should have gone up the steps behind Miles and pushed him down the slide to get him back for the pool incident in Quimper.

Once refreshed from their fun in the pool, Aggie and Miles headed to Saint Brieuc to explore the town. Parking had been easier than she had expected for a town the size of Saint Brieuc and they had even managed to find a space near the cathedral. Perfect.

Aggie and Miles walked through the large wooden doors to the fortress looking Cathédrale Saint Étienne in Place du Général du Gaulle. Aggie wandered over to a display of pamphlets on the cathedral and found one in French and looked at it's map. She then walked slowly around the cathedral looking at the stained glass windows and different chapels until she found the Chapelle des Reliques and the relic of Saint Brieuc. Aggie stopped and looked at the different aspects of the chapel and reflected on her fear of poverty which she felt was connected to her fear of the future. Even though she had struggled in recent years to find a direction with her art, she was now making good progress with her sketches and she felt sure she had enough ideas for a substantial exhibition. This new style could easily be translated into an exhibition of works of Kent and, therefore, would appeal to Kent galleries. That should take care of her worries about the future and money. Was it really that simple, she wondered. She would still have to fight this fear right through until after her next successful exhibition and possibly beyond. It would be an uphill battle fighting this fear. She would have to train herself to ignore any negative critique that would undoubtedly float around in her mind as she prepared this new body of work for exhibiting. She would have to plan a detailed marketing campaign and stick to it. This was what she hated as she was liable to become disorganised and forget to send out press releases and tweet enough to generate the interest she needed in her work. She had done it successfully in the past. She had been on local radio and TV talking about her art. She could do it again. She knew she could. However, she still had a lack of confidence and wondered if this was an age thing. Perhaps this was a normal part of being an artist. Aggie found a pew and sat down to pray for more guidance and also for her family and friends. She couldn't forget them. They were important to her.

Meanwhile, Miles was exploring the cathedral and taking photographs. He was building up a good stock of photographs and sketches for his A'level art. He knew that this particular exam was going to be very demanding and he wanted to make sure he had enough material to relieve the pressure during term time.

Having visited the cathedral, Aggie and Miles found a quiet café and sat down at an outside table. After looking at the menu and placing an order, Miles took off his headphones and looked receptive to a conversation.

"This is very pleasant and civilised," said Aggie as a conversation starter.

"Yeah. The French birds are not bad," came Miles' reply as he surveyed a group of pretty French teenage girls walking past the café.

"I always think French men look more attractive and stylish than Englishmen," said Aggie as she eyed up a rather dapper Frenchman sitting a few tables away. There was something rather attractive about a man in a well-tailored suit and smartly polished shoes.

"Oh come on! You look like a charity shop reject. Look at those shoes!" came Miles' reply knocking Aggie out of her daydream.

Aggie looked at her comfortable five-year-old Ecco shoes that she had worn all holiday. They had been perfect – ideal for wearing with shorts, skirts and jeans. In fact they looked like something Betty would wear. Oh dear. Her dress sense had slipped in the last 20 years. Once upon a time, she would never have dreamt of wearing such shoes. Once upon a time, she wouldn't have dreamt of camping. Once upon a time, she would have been stylishly turned out and wouldn't have looked out of place sitting next to that Frenchman.

After lunch Aggie and Miles drove out of Saint Brieuc to the Plage du Valais overlooking the Baie de Saint Brieuc. The tide was on its way in and they found a quiet spot to sit and take in the views.

Miles took a couple of sheets from Aggie's sketchbook and started to draw.

Aggie sat and stared out to sea, breathing in the fresh smell of sea air. This was how she liked to start her work. There was nothing worse than arriving somewhere in a rush and having to start drawing immediately through the pressure of time. The sky was a vivid blue and there was a light breeze. In the distance Aggie could see storm clouds building. Within a couple of hours the sky had changed completely and there was a chill in the air.

Having decided to pack up they did so quickly and within metres of reaching the car they could feel the first heavy drops of rain. By the time Aggie had reversed out of her parking slot the heavens had opened.

Once back at the campsite Miles decided that it would be a good idea to go for another swim. All the campers had left the pool at the first sign of rain. This was the best time to swim for Aggie and

Miles. They had the pool to themselves and Aggie swam methodically up and down the pool concentrating on her strokes, her breathing and the sound of the water as it lapped around her moving body. There was something almost spiritual about swimming in the rain.

Miles, on the other hand, wasn't interested in spirituality. He was bored. There was no-one to chat to or play with. Oh how he hated that term 'to play with' now that he was almost an adult. He was bored of the slide having spent time on it in the morning. He needed to be creative. The white plastic sun loungers could be put to good use. He wondered if they could float so put one in the pool – it sank. Aggie swam past him and ignored him. It was best to pretend he was nothing to do with her – even though she admired his ingenuity. Aggie firmly believed that boredom was good for creativity. Miles hauled the sun lounger out of the pool and tried to rest it on the edge of the pool. That worked. Then he got onto it and it acted like a slide and he slid into the pool. This was better than nothing so he continued with the game.

Aggie was getting seriously cheesed off with the regular trips to the supermarket. They were running out of inspiration for meal ideas. It was after a particularly boring meal that Aggie sent Miles to do the washing-up while she went to the 'laverie' to wash their clothes. Thankfully, there was a free machine and she had just loaded it with dirty clothes, while muttering to herself about the cost of laundry washing at campsites, when an enthusiastic English woman in her thirties walked in and started loading up the other free machine. They got chatting and Aggie told her about her work as an artist. To Aggie the woman came across as particularly opinionated and full of herself and her work as a marketing manager. She claimed to know anyone who was anyone. She then turned to Aggie and asked her if she was happy being a "poor, struggling artist". Aggie had said she was which was her standard answer to such an annoying question. Thankfully, by this time Aggie's laundry was both washed and dried as she couldn't face what might become an interrogation and critique of her life choices.

That night, as Aggie lay in bed reflecting on the question in a meditative state, she began to realise that the answer had come from her heart and she would always adapt her lifestyle to retain that enjoyment. She enjoyed working with other artists and participating in group events even when the odd artist was difficult. She enjoyed combining art with her sons and how their creativity had fed into her work. Fundamentally, she was happy. No, happy wasn't the word. It was contentment which, to her mind, was a much calmer word. As she lay there, she thought about how it had taken a holiday and running out of funds to be able to see more clearly. If she were to get a part time paid job it would have to work with her and not against her art and family life.

Aggie thought about the woman in the 'laverie' and wondered if she had been content in her chosen career. From what she knew about marketing it could be cut throat. Aggie reflected that she needed to think more kindly on those who asked stupid questions. The questions could just be a reflection of their own problems or inadequacies.

Week 3 – day 15 – Saint Brieuc

Sitting outside the tent enjoying a particularly delicious boulangerie croissant, Aggie decided it was time to brace herself for a new experience. Miles and Aggie were going to take the bus from the campsite into town. She had no idea how the bus system worked and hoped it was easy to buy an 'aller retour'.

Just as she was going to get Miles to stir his stumps she received a text.

> Sally – I have forwarded your fabulous sketches to my friend, Sophie, who runs a boutique art gallery in Saint Malo. As soon as I hear anything I will let you know. Sophie is lovely and I know she will fall in love with your work.
>
> Aggie – Thank you so much. It would be great to get my work into a French gallery.
>
> Sally – My pleasure! Have a great day.
>
> Aggie – You too!

Feeling more optimistic after Sally's text, Aggie sorted out the washing-up after breakfast while Miles got dressed. They then set off on foot from the campsite and walked the short distance to the bus stop.

Aggie was thrilled to have another day of sunshine and an opportunity to rest. Miles had persuaded her to go to the campsite pool as he was hopeful of meeting other teenagers. Aggie agreed to do this in the afternoon as she was inspired to visit some art galleries in the morning.

Once on the bus, Aggie managed to buy the tickets but then caused havoc when she tried to follow the bus driver's instructions on how to get the tickets stamped. Miles stood behind her getting more and more embarrassed. His mother could be so trying at times. It was at moments like this that he wished she was sophisticated and not poor and bohemian. Then they would have eschewed the bus and 'new experience' and driven their Mercedes into town. They wouldn't have a Vauxhall Corsa that was falling apart around them. He imagined the comfort of the Mercedes seats and the refreshingly cool air conditioning.

Finally, the tickets were stamped and Aggie found a seat on the right had side of the bus. Miles decided to sit behind her so he could admire the attractive French girl on the seat behind him. There was an advantage to public transport, he thought, at last.

Miles decided to act cool and sat at an angle with his back to the window and his left leg taking up the adjacent seat so that he could surreptitiously glance at the girl from time to time and smile at her. He hoped his smile didn't look too goofy. He wondered if she was on holiday.

Eventually, he plucked up the courage to speak.

"Salut!" he started simply.

"Salut!" came the reply.

"Je m'appelle Miles."

"Je m'appelle Helène," came the reply with a smile.

148

Miles smiled back and hoped he could muster up enough French for a decent conversation. Aggie was listening in but didn't turn around. She smiled.

"J'ai seize ans," continued Miles, cringing at the basic nature of the conversation.

"Moi aussi. Vous-êtes anglais?" came the reply. Phew thought Miles, relieved that she was making an effort with the conversation.

"Oui, vous habitez ici?"

"Oui. This is my stop," came the reply. "It was nice to meet you," she said, giving him her Instagram name as she got up to go.

"It was nice to meet you too," replied Miles, disappointed that she was leaving but thrilled that he had a means of contacting her. He hoped to meet her again and wondered if he could persuade his mother to spend next years' holiday in Saint Brieuc.

Feeling more cheerful now that he had 'pulled', Miles got out his phone and sent a text to his brother. Richard would be impressed, he thought.

> Miles –Wagwan bitch! Guess what? I've pulled a fit
> French bird on the bus.

> Richard – Good thing I wasn't there!

Now that Miles had forgotten about Aggie's embarrassing ticket stamping, he turned to face the back of her head. She was looking out of the window at the passing street scene. Moving his face to within centimetres of her ear he made a popping sound. Aggie smiled. Miles then did the same with the other ear.

"Donkey!" exclaimed Aggie echoing Shrek's words from the second Shrek film. A fleeting thought crossed her mind that she should probably stop him from doing this and other pranks. One day he might give someone a heart attack. Then, she reflected, life would be so boring without these little interludes.

Aggie's phone beeped to alert her of an incoming text.

Sally – Great news!

Aggie – Really? What?

Sally – I have got you a meeting with Sophie at the gallery in Saint Malo. I will email you with the details.

Aggie – Thank you soooo much.

Sally – My pleasure! Keep me posted.

Aggie – Will do! Have a great day.

Aggie was now feeling more relaxed as they wandered around Saint Brieuc looking at architecture and taking in the feel of the place. Wandering down one of the narrow streets they came across a gallery showing photographs by Michel Lagarde. Standing in the street looking at a photograph in the window Aggie was mesmerised by the attention to detail in it. She enjoyed the humour and marvelled at how the use of clever black and white printing added to the drama of the image. She wished she knew more about photography. Had the image been primarily created 'in camera' or had the photographer used photoshop to its maximum capacity?

Enjoying other art forms was very important to Aggie. They inspired her and fed her imagination. Michel Legarde's photographs had humour in them and were in a style that she wouldn't replicate in her paintings but they took her to another world. Humour and comedy had played a big part in her life.

Once back at the campsite, they headed straight to the pool. Aggie lay on a sun lounger reading her book, glancing up from time to time to watch Miles as he practiced his chat up technique on an 18-year-old girl sitting on her own at the side of the pool. She was reminded of the time when he was 10 years old and they were on a campsite in northern France. She had watched him, then, as he had followed two 14-year-old girls out of the pool and ran after them asking if they had a boyfriend. One had said yes and then turned to her friend and said "tell him you have one too!" Poor Miles. Aggie wondered if he would have more luck this time.

Miles spent a happy hour in the pool with the other teenagers until the girl was called away by her parents. With the main focus of his interest having departed, Miles wandered over to his mother and dripped water onto her bare legs.

"Has anyone ever said you have beautiful legs?" he asked.

"No."

"I am not surprised!"

With that Aggie leapt off her sun lounger and pushed Miles into the pool and then dive bombed him. They both laughed and then got out of the pool and headed back to the tent.

In a bid to avoid the supermarket, Aggie and Miles then headed out to the beach at Valais for chips and an evening of drawing and painting until the sun went down. They both tried to capture the rapidly changing colours of the sunset and, in failing to do so, ended up flicking paint at each other until it was time to head back to the campsite.

It was dark when they arrived back at the campsite, so it was straight to bed. Just as Aggie was about to switch off her torch, her phone pinged to indicate an incoming text.

> Celia – How are you doing? Still feeling sore over Doug?
>
> Aggie – No. Starting to feel a lot more positive. More importantly, have you had a date with Brussels sprout man?
>
> Celia – Ahh! I am in love! We had a fantastic first date. He was so sweet and walked me back to my car. I was looking forward to a passionate embrace to end the date but unfortunately there were a group of teenagers lurking by my car so I was thwarted.
>
> Aggie – Oh no! The perils of dating as an older woman.
>
> Celia – I am glad you didn't say 'middle aged'!
>
> Aggie – LOL. When are you seeing him again?
>
> Celia – Sadly, I have to wait 2 weeks. He is away on holiday.

Week 3 – day 16 – Saint Brieuc

Packing up the tent and leaving Saint Brieuc, Aggie was acutely aware of the trip coming to an end. She was still not sure if she would arrive home a new woman. Would she have the strength of character to stand up for herself as she had hoped the trip would give her? Certainly, she had the beginnings of a promising new style of work. Would Sally's art gallery contact be of use? Would she have any suggestions of where she could market her pictures of Brittany? She hoped she wouldn't tell her that she needed to make another trip to trawl around a hundred galleries at great expense.

Travelling down one of the smaller roads, Aggie ignored the sat nav as it tried to take her onto the autoroute. For some reason it had started to refuse to acknowledge that an autoroute was a motorway. Aggie decided to choose a route and as they were making their way down one of the more rural road, the oil light pinged on. Aggie groaned. She pulled into the gateway to a field and pulled the button to pop open the bonnet of the car. Filling the oil tank she vowed to replace the car when she got back to the UK. There was no way she was going to drive to France the following year in such an unreliable car.

The journey to Saint Malo was silent as they both reflected on nearing the end of their pilgrimage. At the back of Miles' mind were the worries of his GCSE results and starting sixth form. They made a detour to Saint Jacut de la Mer for a wander around the seaside village. Here, Aggie reminisced about childhood holidays to the area and chatted to Miles about the fun she had had rock pooling or building sandcastles on the beach. Those had been simpler times which Aggie had tried to recreate for the boys on their summer holidays.

Heading on and into Saint Malo, Aggie was relieved that she had chosen a campsite on the western fringes of the town. The campsite at Aleth was a small municipal site with sea views and small tidy pitches.

As Aggie hauled the tent out from the back of the car for the last time she felt a mixture of relief and sadness. Relief that this would be the last time the air beds would have to be pumped up and sadness at the thought of leaving France. Just as Miles was positioning the tent, the English woman from the next door pitch came over to say hello and offer a cup of tea. Aggie accepted the offer and, followed the woman over to her caravan while continuing to chat to her. Seeing the car license plate letters were similar to her own Aggie asked if the woman was from Kent.

"Yes," replied the woman, holding up the packet of Kentish tea, saying: "and this is tea from my village, Pluckley. My name is Sarah, by the way."

"Aggie."

Aggie and Sarah became so engrossed in their conversation and the discovery of mutual acquaintances that Miles was forgotten about until he had finished erecting the tent and had come over for his cup of tea.

Having finished their tea, Aggie and Miles went in search of an Intermarche and supper. On returning to the campsite, they then followed the advice of Sarah and took their food and picnic blanket directly to a viewpoint on the Aleth peninsular. From here, they had a vantage point overlooking the port with Saint Malo as a backdrop. Sitting on the picnic rug, they tore the flesh off the roast chicken with their fingers while watching the movement of the port traffic. Beyond the hubbub of the port lay the walled city of Saint Malo, serene in the afternoon light. As they ate their meal they talked of the future and how Miles could set up an online shop and sell his art. Aggie told him about how to approach promoting his work and the best way to get it to work around his studies. Miles enjoyed these conversations with his mother. The opportunity to have these discussions at home and be in the right frame of mind for them was difficult to find. At home there were the distractions, phone calls, homework and so on.

Finishing their chicken, they moved on to eat fresh tomatoes and then Aggie broke a cucumber in half and they ate that. This was one of the best meals, thought Aggie, no washing-up afterwards. They finished with two ripe juicy white peaches with velvety skins. Biting into the whole peaches had the juice running down their chins so they both wiped their faces on their t-shirts. They had become quite slovenly.

Week 3 – day 17 – Saint Malo

Sitting outside the tent on her little camping chair enjoying the peaceful sound of the gas stove heating up the water for her coffee, Aggie was woken from her blissful state of calm by Miles.

"I am just off to build a beaver dam," said Miles as he appeared from the tent.

"What does that mean?" asked Aggie, having a feeling she could guess but still in the early morning pre-coffee fug to be able to xercise her brain.

"Despatch a train."

"Sorry."

"Giving birth to a black eel." Miles was mystified that this mother was so slow. Was she going senile? Perhaps it was because she hadn't had a coffee.

"I beg your pardon." What was Miles on, wondered Aggie as she poured boiling water onto ground coffee and inhaled the rich aroma.

"Having a shit."

"Darling that is such a wide vocabulary you have for 'going for a poo.'"

"You have always encouraged me to have a broad vocabulary."

"I know but I was thinking more in the terms of stuff you could use in your GCSE English exam."

"Oh, but I did."

"No!"

"Yeah, I got in five different expressions for having a shit in my English language paper," replied Miles, proudly, and with that, he confidently trotted off to the sanitary block.

"Oh shit!" said Aggie at the horror of potential re-sits or retaking the year which would ruin her now developing ideas for when Miles had left home.

The walk into town was only a matter of a few kilometres and wasn't hampered by the build-up of traffic that crawled towards the car parks outside the town wall. They briefly stopped at the marina to look at the moored sailing boats and take photos. Aggie took a couple of selfies for her online dating profile, trying to hide her tie-dye t-shirt in the process.

Walking into the cathedral, Aggie felt, as she had walking into the other cathedrals, the feeling of a weight having been lifted from her shoulders. It was as if a group of angels were carrying off her worries. As she stood at the back of the cathedral she wondered what worry was being carried off this time. Fear? No, it wasn't fear. Okay, perhaps it was. But fear of what, she wondered. That certainly covered all the areas she had come to France to solve. She was now single and that was a step forward – or was it backwards, she wasn't quite sure. However, she now had the freedom to make decisions without criticism or having obstacles placed in her way. This was definitely a positive step. She also had a new body of work and that was positive. She had ideas for earning money and she had spent quality time with Miles. She had started Richard off on his first steps to flying-the-nest by leaving him at home for three weeks. Perhaps the problem was that she felt she should be fearful. Perhaps fear had become so ingrained in her that she felt lost without it. She now needed to let go of the fear and embrace the future and new challenges. With that thought, she felt even more weight taken from her.

Finding a quiet pew, she sat down and prayed. She thanked God for helping her gain insight and for all her friends and family. Once again, a peaceful glow swept over her and she remained sitting in the pew for some minutes after having finished praying.

Leaving the cathedral, Aggie and Miles were horrified at the heaving mass of tourists milling around Place Jean de Châtillon and main streets just inside the city walls. Where had they all come from in the time they had been in the cathedral, wondered Aggie. Looking more closely, they appeared to be all from various different coach tours.

Although Aggie was starting to feel more energised, the sight of the vast body of people drained her instantly, so there was only one thing to do in such circumstances. Find a café. They dived into the first café they came across and sat at one of the outdoor tables. As they sat down a grumpy waiter plonked a menu down in front of them and walked off past a man seated at a nearby table who called out "soif" to him. The waiter returned to Aggie and Miles with his order pad, ignoring the man who repeated "soif". The waiter asked what Aggie and Miles wanted. Aggie asked for a coffee and hot chocolate with her best French accent and the waiter looked at her uncomprehendingly. So, Aggie repeated her order more slowly. Aggie could hear the thirsty man call out "soif" again as she spoke. She was just about to ask the waiter if he would prefer her to speak in English or German when he walked off, ignoring the calls of "soif, soif".

Miles looked at Aggie.

"What was wrong with him?" he asked.

"He went to the Paris School of Waiting," replied Aggie.

By the time they had finished their drinks, it was time to head to the gallery. Aggie was nervous. She knew her art was good and she had sold well, but bringing a sketchbook of new images, a new style to a new marketplace was nerve wracking. She had no idea if the owner would like her work 'in the flesh' even though the owner had told Sally that she 'loved' the early sketches Sally had sent to her. Since then Aggie had fleshed out her sketchbook. She had added colour by using the inks and some supermarket crayons. The effect was bold and refreshing, but they might not be suitable for this Breton gallery frequented by wealthy Parisian tourists.

Going into auto pilot in a bid to calm her nerves, they walked confidently into the gallery. Before approaching the reception desk, Miles and Aggie had a look at the paintings in the gallery. The exhibition was of more traditional landscapes in oil. Aggie's heart began to sink. Her new work was so far removed from these paintings that she decided to slink out of the gallery without speaking to the owner. Just as they were making for the door she was approached by a stylishly dressed woman.

"Bonjour, vous-êtes Aggie?"

"Oui," said Aggie, thinking 'oh shit'.

"I am Sophie, Sally's friend."

They shook hands and Aggie introduced Miles and they were led to a back office where Aggie showed Sophie her sketches.

"I am not sure my work is suitable for your gallery," ventured Aggie.

"The images Sally sent were excellent," replied Sophie. "I have just taken over the gallery and am going to shake things up. The current exhibition was okayed by the last owner so I was honour-bound to go ahead with it."

Aggie opened up her sketchbook on Sophie's desk and talked her through the sketches.

"They are even better 'in the flesh'," marvelled Sophie. "How do you see them in an exhibition?"

"Well, they will be predominantly oil on canvas. I was thinking of doing a group of 5 large scale canvases which would draw in the public but would not be affordable to anyone but a serious collector. Then I would do a series of smaller ones at a mid-price point and then some small ones which give a flavour of the large paintings. These would possibly be in pastel and these would be under 100 euros each. I would also have greetings cards or postcards printed of my favourite paintings," replied Aggie.

"This is impressive. You have even thought of the sales side. That makes my life so much easier. Have you thought about the pricing of the medium and large paintings?"

"No, I thought I would leave that up to you as this is a new market I am trying to break into."

"That is good. I will look at that side and get back to you. I can definitely offer you gallery space, but not for a year, unless I get a cancellation. In fact, there is a possibility of a cancellation next year. How does next July sound to you?"

"Perfect," replied Aggie, not quite able to believe her ears. "That gives me enough time to work on the paintings." Aggie was amazed at the speed and ease of the negotiation.

"I will send you a contract via email. I also work with a gallery in Vannes and one in Quimper and I think they would also be interested in your work. It would be good if we could make this a touring exhibition. How does that sound to you?"

"Amazing," was all Aggie could say. This would mean that they would be back in Brittany next summer. Miles had been sitting quietly in the corner listening to music on his phone and suddenly picked up on the atmosphere. Positive vibes all around, he thought, this might mean they could go for a crepe, or even better, two.

Aggie and Miles found the crowded streets of Saint Malo too much to bear, so headed back out of the town to collect the car. They drove inland on local roads that followed the route of the Rance River and stopped at Saint Suliac. Here they found a creperie with river views for lunch. The meal was a celebration for a successful meeting.

As they perused the menu, they chatted about Richard and past meals in creperies. Miles reminded Aggie of her excellent ability to misread menus.

"Remember the time you ordered 'chocolate noix' thinking it was a Nutella type crepe for Richard?"

"Oh yes! The 'noix' stood for 'noix de coco' translating as 'coconut'. Poor Richard. It is the one thing he truly hates."

"I have still not forgotten the time you ordered me a quiche with maroilles."

"It was very tasty."

"You told me it was a type of field mushroom."

"I was having a senior moment and forgot it was a particularly smelly cheese."

"You seem to be having a lot of these senior moments."

"That is because I have you two to bring up."

"Drag up more likely!"

"Thanks!" replied Aggie, laughing and knowing that Miles didn't really mean it.

After lunch, Aggie and Miles found a quiet spot on the sandy banks of the river. There was a gentle breeze and the clouds added interest to the sky.

Aggie used their newly settled position to send a quick text to Sally.

> Aggie – Thank you soooo much for introducing me to Sophie at the gallery. She has offered me an exhibition space – possibly next year!

Sally – That's brilliant! Well done! I knew you could do it! I will come to the private view. Can't wait to see you again.

Aggie – It looks like it will be a touring exhibition so there will be more than one!

Sally – Even better!

The rest of the afternoon was spent making the most of being able to sketch 'plein aire'. They had both taken a large number of photographs to work from once they returned home. However, there was nothing like sitting outside drawing or painting. When it wasn't raining or windy there was a spiritual quality to it. Both Aggie and Miles wanted to make the most of the opportunity.

They started off creating simple watercolour landscapes of the scene and then moved onto rapid sketches of families on the beach. By six o'clock their hands were covered in a mixture of charcoal and brightly coloured pastels. Their stomachs were rumbling, so Aggie went back to the car to fetch the cool box, gas stove, food and water.

After washing their hands, Miles set up the gas stove while Aggie made up some ham and cheese sandwiches. She buttered the outside of one of them and put it in the frying pan, butter side down. Miles lit the stove and fried the sandwich on either side making it into a simple croque monsieur before depositing it onto his plate. Aggie did the same for her croque monsieur and then they savoured their meal while looking out across the river. There were still people rowing or sailing on the river and they both enjoyed watching others hard at work.

Journey by Liz Garnett

One family started to pack up their belongings. Miles watched as one of the older children gave his younger brother a piggy back. Miles thought back to their last family holiday when Richard had still been willing to give him a lift. That had been fun. It had also been fun play fighting and practicing their karate moves on each other. They had been the only children on one particular campsite 'fighting'. Miles had been relieved that Aggie had let them continue and not instructed them to 'behave'.

While Miles was watching the family, Aggie reflected on how nice it had been not to having access to Facebook or Twitter. She regarded Facebook as the worst with its snarky comments on the village community page. She was also relieved that she hadn't been faced with friends photos showing their lovely villa holidays. It would have highlighted the difficult times they had had on their trip. She had managed to keep a check on her car stresses. Now that they were close to their last destination she could relax. If they broke down after Dol de Bretagne, they would be driven straight home on a tow truck and by that time they would have completed their pilgrimage.

Miles and Aggie headed back to the campsite after their supper, both exhausted after their busy day. An early night was much needed.

Week 3 – day 18 – Saint Malo

Packing up the tent for the last time, sadness washed over Aggie. They were nearing the end of their journey. Going back to reality. She knew that life back in England would be just as it had been when she had left and it was up to her to use her new found strength and energy to forge ahead with her work and personal life.

Clambering into the sleeping compartment, Aggie pulled out the plugs on her air mattress and watched it make a huge sigh of relief as it deflated. She repeated the process for Miles' mattress and then started to pack up her mattress by flattening the head end and folding it in stages to force the remaining air out. She wasn't going to miss the airbeds. She did the same for the other mattress and then hauled them both out of the tent and chucked them into the back of the car. She then set about folding up the bedding for the last time. Having not been washed for nearly three weeks it was all starting to smell distinctly feral. Miles' sleeping bag almost had the ability to walk to the car itself. Aggie gave up on the idea of putting the bedding back into it's allotted bag in preference for packing it flat on top of the air beds in the boot of the car. She hoped that the car didn't break down as she piled the bedding on top of where the spare wheel was housed.

Leaving Saint Malo and heading for Dol de Bretagne had been easy. The journey was short and a relief for Aggie who was starting to get fed up of all the driving. Finding the farm where they would spend their last two nights was another matter. They spent a good hour driving around the same rural lanes around Dol trying to find the farm with the sat nav refusing to cooperate. The outside air temperature was pushing 30 degrees and driving slowly on the rural roads was causing the inside air temperature to rise above this.

Having the windows wound down didn't help particularly. Rivulets of sweat poured down Aggie's back and between her breasts.

Eventually, with the help of a detailed IGN walking map and numerous stops in farm entrances to get their bearings, they found themselves driving down a bumpy farm track. They were heading towards the farm where they had booked a yurt for their final two nights.

They pulled into the farmyard and got out of the car. All around them they could hear farm animals and see chickens going about their business. Calling out to the owner with a loud "bonjour" brought out the farmer's wife from one of the barns carrying a basket of freshly laid eggs.

After a brief introduction in French, Aggie and Miles were shown to their yurt which was standing on its own in a field. This was the first time they had stayed in a yurt as Aggie had wanted to end their 'pilgrimage' with something special. The front steps of the yurt looked out onto a meadow with alpacas and a couple of sheep.

Aggie was given a tour of the yurt. Inside was furnished with a large wooden double bed which had been painted in orange and decorated with a series of swirly patterns. It matched the single sofa bed and was the same colour as the wooden beams which held the structure up. There were a couple of old chairs, a small fridge, a small wood burning stove, a table and a series of old rugs spread across the wooden floor. The walls were a simple cotton fabric in cream that hid most of the wooden structure. It had a distinctly ethnic feel to it. The bed and sofa were covered with patchwork quilts and mismatched cushions. After receiving instructions on how the door fastenings worked, Aggie was then shown the shower and toilet which were in a wooden structure near the gate. Once the farmer's wife had left them, Aggie set about putting on the kettle. Miles wandered over to chat to the alpacas and watch some chickens who had appeared in the field. The whole scene was very restful for Aggie to watch as she sat back on the sun lounger and drank her tea.

Aggie – We are doing our last supermarket shop today. What would you like me to bring back for you?

Richard – Harribo Bananas, Le Fermier yoghurt, nice cheese, nice biscuits, paprika crisps, salami, jambon de bayonne, some French films, Batons de Berger, Pineau de Charantes x 4, Pastis x 3, proper French beer x lots, lots of cheap gin for Betty to make sloe gin, absinthe, vodka as well, pistachios, syrops – lots of different flavours but not mint, lots of chocolate but not the cheap supermarket chocolate, lots of nougat.

Aggie – Who is paying for that lot?

Richard – Pretty please??????

Aggie – I may not get all of it. I am running out of cash.

Richard – I will do your gardening for you.

Aggie – I think you still owe me ten hours in the garden as it is.

Richard – I need supplies for university.

Aggie – You will end up with scurvy if those are
your supplies for university!

Walking into the supermarket at Dol, Aggie made a mental note to buy anything she needed for the next couple of days, along with goodies to take back to the UK. Miles followed her in and made his way to the customer service desk to ask for a 'jeton' (token) for the trolley. He wanted to make sure there was enough room for his biscuits and other goodies. If his mother picked up the basket on wheels there would be no way he would get half of what he wanted. His mission was to go directly to the biscuit aisle and get in as much as he could before Aggie noticed. That was one of the good things about his mother. In a French supermarket he could choose pretty much what he wanted as long as it was French and he couldn't get it in the UK. This had been their holiday rule for as long as he could remember. If he wanted a particular cake in a patisserie he could have it as long as he spoke French. This was the one time when money appeared to be no object. Although, he had noticed that meals at home had a distinct budget quality to them for a good number of months after a holiday. He wondered how many months it would take Aggie to balance the books this time.

Miles decided to make a good exploration of the supermarket. He didn't want to miss anything and while he was wending his way up and down the aisles, he came across a lobster tank by the fish counter. He spent some minutes watching the lobsters moving about and was reminded of a past holiday with Richard. Dear Old Richard was always good at coming up with fun things to do. On this one particular occasion he had bet Miles £10 to put his hand in the tank and pick up a lobster. What a hoot, thought Miles. It was such a shame the fishmonger had stopped him. Knowing that Aggie was game for a laugh he wondered, briefly, if she would bet him the £10 but then realised that she may be a bit short of funds after three weeks away.

Miles got out his phone, took a photo of the lobsters and sent it to Richard.

> Miles - £20 to dare me to put my hand in and pick one up.
>
> Richard - £5.
>
> Miles - £15.
>
> Richard - £10 and I need to see evidence.
>
> Miles – Deal.

Just as Miles was about to put his hand in the tank, Aggie caught sight of what was about to happen and stood back. She was just about to surreptitiously video the act when the fishmonger came over and stopped Miles. Aggie disappeared in the direction of the vegetable aisle and Miles, seeing her flee the scene, followed after her. He caught up with her beside the tomatoes.

"How much did Richard dare you to do that?" asked Aggie, knowingly.

"£10."

"That was a bit tight of him."

They both started to laugh before Aggie sent a text to Richard.

Aggie – Stop encouraging your brother to be naughty. He got caught.

Richard – Soz.

Aggie and Miles spent the rest of the day at the yurt enjoying an opportunity to rest. It was also an opportunity to have their first ice cream of the summer. They lay on the sun loungers outside the yurt watching the alpacas while tucking into large quantities of Carte d'Or coconut ice cream. Miles had added chocolate sprinkles and gummy bears to his.

As Aggie clambered into bed, she took a moment to breathe in the fresh smell of the bed linen. She savoured the sensation of lying between clean sheets on a proper bed. Miles' response to getting into a proper bed with freshly laundered sheets was not the same. To him, the smell of the bed linen wasn't as welcoming as the smell of week-old sheets that had absorbed his unique aroma.

Week 3 – day 19 – Dol de Bretagne

It had been pure bliss finally to spend a night in a proper bed with proper sheets. The sheets had smelt fresh and clean. Aggie had only needed one trip to the toilet in the night and that had almost been spiritual. The air had been cool and dry and she had heard the hoot of two owls as she made her way to the wooden shed housing the toilet. Before going back into the yurt, she had stopped at the yurt door to take in the smell of the countryside and the sounds of the farm animals moving about in the field. As she climbed into bed, the bells had chimed the hour on a nearby church. This was what was missing from village life back in Kent.

Aggie turfed Miles out of bed at 8 am so that they could go and have breakfast in the farmhouse kitchen. The kitchen was a traditional working farm kitchen with a large range. Taking up most of the floorspace of the kitchen was a large wooden table laid out for a hearty breakfast. It was a treat for them to drink their morning coffee out of traditional 'bols' and to chat in French about life in Brittany and compare French and English politics. It had been pure bliss to eat fresh baguette spread with homemade butter and jam. The croissants had melted in their mouths and both Miles and Aggie had been rendered speechless as they ate them. The quatre quarts loaf cake had a deep yellow colour given to it by the recently laid farm eggs. It had been made fresh that morning and still retained warmth from the oven.

Walking into the Cathédrale de Saint Samson, Aggie was immediately struck by the light streaming in through the stained glass window at the far end of the cathedral. There was a comforting air about the place. She looked up and marvelled at the feat of architectural design that had led to such a high roof structure.

Walking around the cathedral, Aggie had a sudden moment of panic. She eventually found the relics of Saint Samson in a small chapel and stood soaking up the scene. Even though she had begun to feel as if she had made progress and would be returning home with a sense of purpose, Aggie felt panic stricken. Had she really made progress? Had she spent the last of her savings on a holiday that would have her back at square one when she got home? Aggie hated all the self-doubt that was causing havoc with her mind.

A priest approached her, guessed that she was from England and started speaking to her in English.

"Hello, can I help you?" asked the priest.

"That is very kind of you," replied Aggie, who then went on to tell him about her journey. "So, you see, I had hoped to end the pilgrimage with some insight or having changed in some way. I just feel as though nothing has changed."

"You have made a pilgrimage and, even though it isn't on foot, you have made modern day sacrifices like giving up sleeping under a roof and all the comforts of living in a modern day house. Pilgrimage comes from the Roman word peregre which means journey. You have certainly had a journey and you have overcome difficulties. You are being too hard on yourself. Your journey didn't start the minute you got into your car and drove away from your home. It started before that. Years before. Look at what you have achieved. You have two sons of whom you are proud. They didn't become young men without your help and support.

Journey by Liz Garnett

"As to the last three weeks, you have ended an unsuitable relationship and therefore risked loneliness and loss of the love of another adult. That takes courage. That has now opened up your heart and freed it to find your true love. That free space has also had a chance to welcome in a new style of art and out of that you have been offered gallery space. You have spent quality time with your son and worked on that relationship. From what you have told me, you clearly understand the role of a mother to let your children fly the nest by helping them to reach that point.

"You mustn't forget that art is not a conventional job. Nor is it really a career. It is a passion – a lifelong one very similar to raising children. You never stop being a parent even when the child has left home. Likewise, you never stop being an artist, even when you try to retire."

"Thank you. How do you know and understand all that about being an artist?"

"My mother was an artist," replied the priest. "You have changed, even though you don't see it now. Would you like me to pray with you to help you on your journey?"

"Yes, please."

The Priest and Aggie then knelt in front of the little chapel and prayed together. Once they had prayed, the priest left Aggie to spend some time reflecting on her journey. Seeping into every crevice of her mind was a sense of relief. She had overcome adversity and she was starting to see a clearer future. With her career, she was now well on the way to a new body of work in a refreshingly new style. She would be using her art to run classes from which she could see exciting opportunities with other forms of work once Miles had left home. As to Miles, well, he had decided to re-think his A'level choices and his sketches over the holiday had really progressed into a strong and distinctive style. He was also starting to talk about taking a gap year and felt he now had the confidence to do it on his own. They had both achieved something on this pilgrimage.

Aggie and Miles drove to Cherrueix and parked up just outside the village in a parking area that looked onto the Baie de le Mont Saint Michel. From this quiet spot they had a view of the great pilgrimage site in the distance.

They both sat on the picnic rug and got out their art materials and drew the scene. In the distance, they could see a group of people being guided across the bay. The tide was out and they both quietly watched the slow progress of the walkers.

Reflecting on their journey, Aggie thought about the progress she had made. Her future was now mapped out in the short term and was flexible enough to embrace a new direction should one be presented to her. She felt happier in herself and her newly single status and happier in general.

As she flipped through her sketchbook, she started to see her work in a new light. It was good. It showed real skill - a skill that she had developed over the past 30 years. However, it was lighter, brighter, looser and more free. It was a reflection of who she was becoming. As she sat there looking at her work she fell in love with it for the first time. A passion for it was starting to emerge. She would need this passion and the confidence that it brought going forward as this would help to keep her motivated. She knew that there were some of her contemporaries, back in Kent, who would dislike it. These artists disliked change and were convinced that the only way to be an artist was to develop one style and stick to it. To them, this was how it was to be a professional artist. Aggie hated this controlled and rigid approach to art. She didn't want to be confined to a box. Aggie looked up to artists like David Hockney who embraced changing styles. She wasn't sure she would follow Hockney into creating art using an iPad, though. However, it was his ability to reinvent himself that she admired most and felt this was a necessary approach as an artist. As a child she had grown up listening to the music of David Bowie and Adam and the Ants. As musicians, they had been known for their skill at reinventing themselves with each album. To Aggie this required a huge amount of courage, energy and talent.

Miles looked at his mother. He had started to notice how she had changed over the three weeks. She looked happier and more relaxed. He was pleased that she had dumped Doug. He had been worried that Aggie would want him to move in with them now that Richard was going to University. Miles was relieved. He loved his mother's relaxed style of parenting. When he had friends over they were allowed to take over the sitting room. He had the distinct feeling that Doug would have put a stop to this. Even the parties Aggie threw were more sombre affairs with no party games when Doug was around. Doug also disapproved of Betty and her eclectic mix of homemade gins and vodkas. Life was looking up for Miles.

"Let's have a party when we get home," he said, breaking the silence.

"Great idea. Shall we have one as a send-off for Richard?" replied Aggie.

"Yeah. How many friends can I invite?"

"That will depend on the weather. If we can use the garden then I don't see why you can't have 8 to 10 friends each."

Even though he had 'come along for the ride', the pilgrimage had benefited Miles, too. He had cleared his mind of his GCSE studies and had some really good ideas for earning some filthy lucre while he was in sixth form. He doubted he would have formed any of these ideas if he had stayed in Kent. He was now looking forward to heading home and seeing his friends. Aggie had already given him a timetable of when he could have friends over and when she would be available to drive him to see friends. She was good like that.

Aggie couldn't quite believe that it was their last night. They had completed their pilgrimage and she was determined to celebrate with a meal out at a nice restaurant.

Having showered, she booted Miles out of the yurt so she could have space and privacy to change into her one and only smart dress and high heeled shoes. Once she had applied the finishing touches of make-up she opened the yurt door.

"Ta daah! What do you think?" she asked Miles who was sitting quietly outside soaking up the evening sun.

"Those shoes make you look like a cross between Theresa May and a hooker," came Miles' reply. Aggie raised her eyebrows and realised that Miles wasn't going to change and being a teenage boy what reply had she expected? She wondered, briefly, if a daughter would have been kinder, then she remembered Magda's daughters and their comments on Magda's clothing choices and she realised it must be teenagers full stop.

Aggie and Miles drove into Dol de Bretagne and parked in the main street. It had been a while since Aggie had worn high heels and she was finding it difficult to walk. Miles appraised his mother's appearance as they headed to the restaurant.

"You could be quite a convincing drag queen," he said, taking in her bright red lipstick which co-ordinated beautifully with her red shoes and handbag.

"Do you want a lift home?"

"No, not really. Do you want to go home?"

"No. I would rather be wandering around the French countryside doing my art."

Miles spotted a small restaurant further up the main street and set off at speed leaving Aggie to teeter after him. Miles was starving. He had no intention of admiring the local architecture. When he reached the door of the restaurant, he turned around to see that Aggie was following him and, once he was sure she had seen him, went inside and asked for a table for two in his best French. Within minutes, Aggie had joined him, slightly flushed from her efforts to walk in her smart shoes.

It wasn't until after they had ordered that they realised that the restaurant was half full of English people. Aggie was horrified to listen in on the loud conversations about food and requests for a children's menu in English. Both Miles and Aggie raised their eyebrows at the horror of such a request. To them the menu, in all it's French-ness, offered a perfect combination of both meat and seafood cooked in the local style. Trying to ignore the other diners, they spent a pleasant meal chatting about their journey and laughing at the funny things that had happened en route.

After their meal, Aggie and Miles headed back to the yurt. As the last rays of the sun were fading away, they sat on the sun loungers drinking farm cider and relaxing.

Aggie had found the holiday physically exhausting but also mentally exhilarating. She felt ready to take on the world.

Miles was also worn out and was looking forward to getting home to his Xbox. Aggie had never taken them on a beach holiday and he was convinced she didn't know the meaning of the word 'relax'. He loved her dearly, but he hadn't even had a chance to recover from his marathon of GCSE exams. He knew, from past experience, that he could rely on at least a week or two of post-holiday peace and quiet. Aggie would be too busy doing the washing, mucking out the car and getting on with her work. If Richard had been throwing wild parties and not clearing up, there was hope that the two weeks might extend into three.

Week 3 day 20 – Dol de Bretagne

Miles and Aggie had enjoyed sitting in the farmhouse kitchen eating their petit dejeuner and speaking French. For Aggie, it was a chance to soak up the last morsels of French culture that they would experience for some time, while Miles enjoyed the variety of conversation from politics to life in France.

By the time Aggie and Miles finally left the yurt, it was 10 am. The sky had clouded over. Aggie had checked the weather forecast before breakfast and seen that there was a storm coming in from the west that would either follow them, or sit on top of them, all the way to Calais. She needed to get a move on if she was going to avoid driving in a storm as torrential rain would make her journey difficult. Needless to say, she had been reluctant to get going.

Aggie had been pleased to discover that the yurt had had a small fridge. It had made for a civilised end to their journey and meant that she had been able to do the end-of-holiday supermarket shop on the day they arrived at the yurt. This would save them from a mad dash around Carrefour in Calais or, if they were delayed, missing a final shopping trip altogether. This pre-emptive supermarket shop had resulted in a distinct whiff of Maroilles and Camembert cheeses wafting around the car. This was mingled with smoked garlic and sweaty teenager. Aggie pretended that she wasn't contributing in any way to the smell, even though she was wearing two day old knickers and a three day old t-shirt. She had convinced herself that a liberal dose of French perfume would deal with any of her bodily odours.

By the time they hit the périphérique at Caen, Miles was complaining that his stomach thought his throat had been cut. Aggie had hoped that the large breakfast would sustain them until

Calais, but she hadn't bargained on her son's ability to consume large quantities of food and still be hungry. Her large breakfast coffee was also weighing heavily on her bladder, so they pulled off at the Ifs sortie and headed straight for the Golden Arches, or as the French called it, McDo. This was another American chain of public conveniences that provided filling carbohydrates for Miles and coffee for Aggie. She hated MacDonalds but had to admit they were handy as toilet stops and she could be guaranteed of not having to use a squat toilet.

As they slowed down on the approach to the first tolls after the Caen périphérique, Aggie ran her left hand through her hair and wished she had washed it that morning. The slightly greasy texture was now assisting her hair to stick up in an uncontrollable manner giving her the look of a wild woman. This was a look she knew well and could wear with pride, even though she wished she had hair with more control. An ability to maintain an elegant appearance would be nice, she thought. She hoped she wouldn't bump into anyone she knew on the ferry going home.

After the tolls, Aggie settled into her 'happy place'. Seeing a mother driving five teenage boys in the car behind her at the tolls reminded her of the times when she had picked up her sons and a couple of friends and given them a lift home. Miles had always enjoyed seeing Richard's friends and having them share the back seat of the car meant he had a captive audience. Richard had always had to sit in the front passenger seat in order to prevent any brotherly squabbling. Miles always sat in the middle of the rear passenger seat to aid weight distribution.

Aggie smiled to herself as she remembered one occasion.

"Mother, What is chlamydia?" asked the 10-year-old Miles.

"Darling, I will explain it to you later," came Aggie's reply in a bid to buy time. "Please can we change the subject," she added suspecting that Miles knew very well he was on a censored topic.

Miles then turned to Richard's friend Robert. "Robert, what is chlamydia?"

"Err, I don't know," came Robert's wise response, while Richard tried to stifle a snigger and Aggie tried to concentrate on the road.

Miles then turned to Richard's friend on his right. "Joe, do you know what chlamydia is?"

"Err no," came Joe's diplomatic and embarrassed response.

Aggie then came in with "Miles! Please can we leave this subject alone? I said I would explain later."

This silenced Miles for a few minutes and then he piped up with "Mum, what is syphilis?"

Thinking quickly, Aggie replied "darling that is not how you pronounce it. It is pronounced physalis. It is a fruit that is also known as the cape gooseberry."

"So, it is not syphilis?" said Miles knowing full well his mother knew it was and was working hard to try to outwit him. He was not stupid.

"No," replied Aggie, hoping this would put an end to the subject but fearing that there were quite a few more words in this subject area that he could bring out.

Then, Richard decided to enter into the conversation.

"Miles, Chlamydia is a name frequently given to girls in Essex."

This generated a lot of giggling from Joe and Robert in the back of the car.

Putting on a high pitched girlie voice Richard then said "Chlamydia, oy Chlamydia, go and find your sister, Syphilis!"

The car then erupted in the gales of laughter. Aggie was left wondering how she was supposed to keep a straight face when her sons were so funny.

They were almost at Calais when Aggie's bladder demanded a pit stop. Pulling off at the Aire des Deux Caps, Aggie ran into the service building and was confronted by a queue outside the ladies toilets. She hated waiting in queues, except in France, where she could enjoy some people watching and eavesdropping. Just as she was enjoying a particularly interesting conversation between two friends about another friend's affair, she saw some women decide the queue was too long and watched as they walked confidently into the gents. Only in France, thought Aggie. She decided, on this occasion, to be frightfully British and not follow their lead. Besides, the conversation about the affair was far too enthralling to leave without a conclusion.

Finally, Aggie and Miles reached the Port of Calais and pulled in behind a campervan with brightly coloured paintwork. There were considerable queues of traffic lined up at the French border control booths. French soldiers with machine guns walked between the cars and asked drivers to open up their car boots so they could check for stowaways. A very young soldier, barely out of nappies, indicated to Aggie that he wanted her to get out and open the boot of her car. She got out and he visibly chocked on the fumes that came out with her. She shut her car door and opened the boot. The waft of Maroilles cheese was like a soccer punch and the poor young soldier had to step back and retch before waving her on.

Getting back into the car, Aggie made a mental note to make sure the first port of call, once they were on the boat, was the duty free shop so she could 'test' a good number of perfumes in order to eradicate – or at least attempt to eradicate – the smell she was now carrying with her. She wondered whether she could persuade Miles to do the same with aftershave. On reflection, probably not. However, this could possibly be used to their advantage and perhaps no one would sit anywhere near them.

Reaching the embarkation queues, Aggie found the correct lane and pulled up behind a very smart Mercedes S class. The British number plate indicated it was heading home. It was immaculately clean. Aggie looked around the queues of traffic and saw there were other British cars equally pristine. Clearly, they had been washed at the end of their holiday. What must they all think of her muddy Corsa? She didn't care. She hadn't wasted any of her precious time with her son farting about cleaning her car, she thought.

As they sat patiently waiting for the embarkation call, the heavens opened. Aggie was relieved that they hadn't had to drive through the storm but wasn't looking forward to crossing the channel.

Having boarded the ferry and availed themselves of a good many perfume and aftershave testers, Aggie and Miles left the shop having not bought anything. Reeking of a fine selection of the very best French perfumes and aftershaves, they wandered around the ferry, looking for somewhere quiet to sit. There wasn't anywhere. The boat was packed to the gunwales. Aggie mentally counted up her pennies and decided that there was nothing for it but to go to the smart onboard restaurant.

The ferry started to leave the dock when Aggie and Miles took their seats in the brasserie restaurant. Aggie remembered the days when there were white tablecloths and it was named after a smart London restaurant. Those were the days when you could pretend you were cruising across the channel.

As soon as the ferry left the protection of the harbour walls the ferry started to rock from side to side. Looking out of the window, Aggie could see the white caps on the sea. It was going to be a rough crossing. Aggie had been oblivious of the windy conditions as she had driven up the autoroute to Calais, her mind had been focussed on reaching the ferry on time.

At the neighbouring table, the woman was talking about the rough sea and questioning the safety of the ferry. The husband was reassuring her by saying there were stabilisers. Aggie marvelled at the ignorance of the man, knowing that the stabilisers wouldn't stop the boat from sinking.

Miles' ears pricked up. The woman was clearly anxious. He whipped out his mobile phone and googled ferry disasters in Europe and came up with the Herald of Free Enterprise. Bingo!

"Mum?" started Miles.

"Yes, darling." What was he up to, wondered Aggie, recognising a particular tone in his voice.

"The Herald of Free Enterprise was a roll on roll off ferry like this one, wasn't it?"

"Yes, darling."

"Was it as rough as this when that ferry sank?"

"They hadn't closed the ferry doors when it left the port, darling." Aggie could see where this was going and didn't want to spoil his fun.

From the adjacent table came the quiet but anxious voice of the wife. "Do you think they have closed the doors properly?"

"They learnt from that disaster and have to close the doors before leaving the dock." came the husband's reply.

"They were in quite a rush to make up time," said Miles to Aggie knowing he was onto a winner here. The bad weather had delayed most of the crossings all day.

"Darling, they won't skimp on things like that. They won't be allowed to."

He wasn't getting anywhere here. Mmmm he thought. What could he add to raise his neighbour's anxiety levels?

"What about a terrorist attack?" he asked.

"Darling, they have very good security now."

"Are you sure?"

"Yes," said Aggie starting to feel anxious.

The sea was very choppy and the bow of the boat kept hitting wave after wave with a dull bang.

Thankfully, their meal arrived so Miles was temporarily halted from his disaster train of conversation. As they tucked into their fish and chips and Aggie savoured the taste of chips dunked into thick tartar sauce, Miles started up again.

"They didn't check every vehicle."

"Who didn't?"

"The security chaps."

"They know what to look out for."

"I don't want to die just yet," came Miles' response, in the hope that this would increase the anxiety on the next table.

"You aren't going to die just yet," said Aggie soothingly.

There was an even louder bang as the bow of the ferry hit a particularly large wave.

"What was that bang?" asked Miles, now starting to feel anxious himself.

"It was just a wave."

"Are you sure? It sounded like a bomb going off."

"I am sure." Aggie was finding this conversation very wearing. She had hoped to arrive home relaxed and recharged. The woman on the other table had started to go from white to a pale green colour. Aggie was briefly distracted by wondering what shaded of Windsor and Newton green could be mixed with white to achieve that particular shade of green.

"I haven't even had a cigarette," said Miles warming to the theme. On the next table the husband continued to reassure his wife who was becoming increasingly distressed.

"Miles, Please can we change the subject?"

"If I do die, I want to be buried with my Xbox."

"Why?"

"I want to be able to play on it when I get to heaven."

"Darling, they don't have any electricity up there."

"Yes they do!"

"No they don't!"

"Then I want to go to hell. Betty said she is going there as she thinks it will be more fun than heaven."

"I know she does but she is quite batty, darling."

At the next table a waitress brought a double gin and tonic and the wife downed it in one go and asked for another one. Miles smiled to himself and mentally gave himself a gold star for being successful in scaring the pants off his neighbour.

Pulling into the driveway, Aggie was met by Betty's mobility scooter parked at a jaunty angle. She smiled, thinking how nice it would be to see her aunt and have a hug and a warm welcome after the long journey.

Opening the front door, she realised that it wasn't just her aunt in the house. On the stairs were a couple of teenagers in a passionate embrace. Oh God, she said to herself, I hope no one is copulating in my bed. In the sitting room she saw a group of decidedly merry teenagers sitting on the floor playing a game of Cards Against Humanity. She turned to go into the kitchen and found even drunker teenagers including her son, Richard, daring each other to eat a fresh chilli.

"Oh, hello Mum. What are you doing back today?" came Richard's somewhat slurred greeting.

"I said I would be back today, darling," replied Aggie still trying to get her head around the scene that greeted her.

"Oh right. I thought you would be back tomorrow."

"So, I see. Where's Betty? Her scooter's on the driveway."

"Errr… in the dining room, I think," came Richard's reply who then turned to his friends and laughed as one of them was suffering the consequences of a particularly hot fresh chilli. Aggie regarded the scene and laughed. Stupid boys! They were clearly doing it for the benefit of the two girls who were standing watching the spectacle.

Aggie opened the door to the dining room to find Betty sitting on a beanbag playing Call of Duty on the Xbox with two of Richard's friends. Aggie had no idea how her 80-year-old aunt managed to get onto the beanbag and she hoped the boys would help her up off it when she had finished the game.

Quietly shutting the door, Aggie turned her attention to the state of the kitchen. There were half empty bottles of sloe gin and plum vodka with Betty's homemade labels on them. Who was leading who astray, she wondered. Then she caught a glimpse of another unlabelled bottle, this time larger than Betty's. One of Richard's Latvian friends had been raiding his parents homemade drinks supply.

Heading back out of the kitchen, she realised that there was nothing for it, but to go out to the car and start unloading. As she passed the open doorway to the sitting room, she saw that Miles had snuck in and was enjoying a glass of sloe gin as he took his place amongst Richard's friends to join the card game.

Welcome home said Aggie to herself.

About the Author

Liz Garnett is a photographer and writer based in Kent, United Kingdom. She has lived in France and regularly takes her sons to France on holiday or for short trips. Each summer, she combines staying in a mobile home with a few days under canvas. In 2018, Liz followed the route of the Tro Breiz pilgrimage which was the inspiration for this novel. As well as being inspired by the French way of life she hopes to become bilingual one day by continuing to learn the language.

www.lizgarnett.com